Teens Talk
About Fear

Rhonda S. Gladden
Renee S. Talbott

Xulon Press
11350 Random Hills Road
Suite 800
Fairfax, VA 22030
(703) 279-6511
XulonPress.com

To order additional copies, call 1-866-909-BOOK (2665).

About The Authors

Rhonda Gladden and Renee Talbott think so much alike they could be twin sisters, except for the fact that they were born six years apart. Their genuine love for young people has constantly put them in the position of working closely with kids, and has endeared them to teens around the world.

They have been contributing writers and columnists in numerous features magazines; content producer for various nationally known entities (CosmoGirl!, Sears Mainframe Fashion for teens, Boys Town, etc.); and Channel Producer for Talk City's Online "Teen, Kids and College Communities."

Having worked closely with thousands of teens both online and real world, they are very much in tune with the feelings and emotions teens face today. Most importantly, they have a strong desire to see kids rise above adversity and be strong in their faith.

TABLE OF CONTENTS

Foreword

A WORD FROM DR JOE B. BROWN
Senior Pastor, Hickory Grove Baptist Church

Hickory Grove Baptist Church is a 13,000-member church located in Charlotte, North Carolina. In 1996 the church formed a second campus in the northern part of Charlotte.

It's not easy growing up in America today. Things are not as simple as they once were because there is more real danger in our world than ever before.

There is the real threat of sexually transmitted diseases, like aids. We have terrorists killing themselves and everyone around them. Every day our schools are the distribution and selling ground for illegal drugs which paralyze and kill. After the massacre at Columbine, we have a glimpse of the jungle our children traverse everyday.

In the face of these tragic events, I'm reminded that Jesus said our world will be filled with great difficulties and fearful things — but we are not to react in fear. We are to respond in **faith**.

Therefore, it is my privilege to recommend and endorse this book, *"Teens Talk About Fear."* It will enable your teen to identify their fears and learn that **they are not alone with this problem.** Reading the testimonies from teens experiencing the same emotions is somehow comforting, and to hear how someone has overcome in a similar situation is very encouraging.

Each chapter not only has teens expressing their fears and responding to one another, but the authors have put together incredible scriptural references to empower your teens in the face of their fears. The journal sections are designed to help the reader to become healthy and secure in who they are.

I have personally known the authors (Rhonda Gladden and Renee Talbott) for many years. In fact, I have been their pastor for more than 15 years.

I know them to be committed to the **people of God**. Both of the ladies are very talented individuals and they give freely of their time and talent to bring the blessings of God upon the Church of Jesus Christ.

As you read this book, it is my prayer that you will not only get to know the authors, but you will also be blessed by **The Author, Jesus Christ**, who is the creator of all things. It's important for you to realize that of all the people who have ever lived, **you are the only one like you**. God has gone to a great deal of trouble to make sure that **you are one of a kind.**

This book will have been successful if it helps you discover your uniqueness in Jesus Christ. The goal is for you to realize who you are in Christ, and to know with certainty that there is **NO FEAR** in Him!

Finally, I hope that after reading this book, you are more aware of not only **who God is,** but **who you are in Jesus Christ.**

Chapter 1:

FEAR OF ASKING FOR HELP

Teens Talk

Monica (15) shares her fear:

"I'm starting high school and I'm way behind in math. I just don't understand algebra. Everybody else in my class last year laughed at the kids who struggled with it and asked questions, so I just pretended to get it.

Now I've got to take summer classes to move on to the next grade. I know if I ask questions I'm going to look really stupid. If I ask my dad, he'll be mad cuz I don't know what I'm supposed to know. If I flunk it, though, I'll be in even bigger trouble."

Jessica (16) responds:

"Asking for help isn't something I have a problem with,

but here's how I see it. What's more stupid — asking questions, or taking mandatory summer classes? I know I'd rather be laying in the sun than taking classes during summer break! That's a no brainer!"

Tray (15) responds:

"I don't like having the attention on me, so I know how you feel. Asking questions in class means everyone looks at you, and they think "Man, he's stupid!" If I don't feel comfortable asking something in class, I'll ask a friend, or the teacher after class. There's always more than one way to do something."

Aaron (17) responds:

"I was in the exact same situation! I used to be shy and wouldn't say a word in class, but last year I had to go to summer school because I just didn't get English.

"My dad was ticked off when I told him I pretended to understand it 'cause I was too scared to ask questions. I did really well in summer school — everyone in the class was struggling, so we all asked questions. The cool thing was that most of the questions people asked were things that I didn't understand — I wasn't the only one who didn't get it.

"That experience helped me the next year in school 'cause I wasn't quite so shy about asking questions."

Jordan (17) shares her fear:

"I started my first job a couple of weeks ago. It's only part time, but it's great spending money, and I get decent discounts on all the clothes. (I'm a retail sales clerk at a department store.)

"The people I work with are friendly enough, but everyone

is so wrapped up in their own thing, and my boss is kinda short-tempered. He quickly gave me a walk-thru, and then threw me off on another sales clerk to finish my training.

"Most things are easy, but ringing up sales and returns are still frustrating. I can't quite figure out how to void things out, and I get really nervous. I really flubbed up last week and it took two managers to figure out what I'd done wrong on the register. The customer was polite, but I could tell she was getting pretty hacked off at having to wait so long.

"If someone has advice on how to ask for help without looking like a complete idiot, I'd give them my skechers!"

Jim (18) responds:

"My first job was as a sales clerk, too, and I remember being really intimidated the first few weeks. Just learning the cash register was bad enough, but there were the store policies, forms to fill out, location of all the merchandise, etc., etc. I think I was brain dead after the first day!

"My boss was a real jerk, too. She didn't want to answer any questions, and she made me feel really stupid if I didn't understand stuff right away.

"Fortunately, I became good friends with several of the other clerks who had been there for a while, and they took me under their wing. Any time I needed help, they were just a shout away. One of them even stayed late a couple of nights to walk me through problems I'd had that day.

"Eventually, I knew enough to not only do my job, but to help the newbies when they were hired. I kinda made it my duty to help them out. I figured I might need help again someday, and I better start paying my dues now."

Tracie (19) responds:

"I think it's important to be very open and speak your mind when you need to know something. It doesn't matter if it's at school, or work, or wherever.

"My mom had cancer last year and I remember her telling me she had to ask the doctor all kinds of questions. She did research online and even challenged the doctor on some of the information he told her.

"She said 'It's MY life and no one cares more about the quality of my life than ME! If I won't stand up for myself and ask questions, who will?'

"That kind of spunk makes me proud of my mom, and makes me want to be like her. Who cares if someone calls you stupid or acts like you've inconvenienced them if you ask a question? Your boss is being paid to make sure you know how to do your job. Don't let them get by with that kind of lousy attitude.

"I say be bold and ask as many questions as it takes to get your answer!"

Karen (16) responds:

"You rock, Tracie! Way to be in control! I'm gonna follow the advice you gave Jordan and quit being a weenie. Thanks!"

Mike (16) shares his fear:

"I don't know how to get the self-confidence to speak up and ask a question in class when I hate to have everyone look at me."

Sid (17) responds:

"I don't know what to tell you to do except to just step out and DO IT! I mean, there comes a point in time when you just have to suck it up and do whatcha gotta do."

Jill (17) responds:

"Sid, that's easier said than done. Maybe you're not shy, but some of us are. It ain't as easy as you make it sound. I'm not sayin' that you're wrong, but maybe another option is to find someone who can privately answer questions or act as a tutor."

Tracie (19) responds:

*"Ok, here I go again. It's okay to find alternative ways to get something done, but that may not always be possible. Sid is right, sometimes it ain't easy, but sometimes you've gotta just **do it!***

"The key for me was to worry less about what people think about me and be more concerned about what was in my best interest. That's not rocket science."

What The Bible Has To Say

The first thing to realize about asking for help is that every person has to do it at some point in time. It's a natural part of life.

As a child, we ask for help to do things like tying our shoes or climbing the stairs. As a teen we ask help for things like learning to drive a car.

When we become adults, we don't stop asking for help. It might be in work related issues, or advice about securing a home mortgage. As senior-adults, we ask for help with things we may no longer be able to do by ourselves. It's a life-long process.

Even the corporate world has recognized "team work" as one of the most successful concepts. Employees work better as a team because where one person lacks experience or knowledge, another employee picks up the ball and runs with it.

There is nothing to be ashamed of in asking for help. It doesn't mean we are weak, it means that we are strong enough to realize we are still learning.

Isaiah 40:31 says that *"those who wait on the Lord will find new strength. They will fly high on wings like eagles. They will run and not grow weary. They will walk and not faint."*

Turn the fear of asking for help over to God, and He will give you the strength to get through any struggle that you may face. You are never a failure with God on your side.

How Does This Apply To Me?

Have you ever needed help but refused to ask for it? Write down an example.

_____

_____

_____

How did you feel when you didn't accomplish your goal simply because you were afraid to ask for help?

_____

_____

_____

How would you react if a good friend asked for your help?

_____

_____

_____

How can you overcome the fear and get help so that you can accomplish your goals?

_____

_____

_____

Look at the story of Moses from Exodus 17: 8 - 13. Describe how Moses received help.

_____

_____

_____

Had Moses been unwilling to accept help, the Israelites would have been defeated. Do you see this as a weakness on Moses' part? Why or why not?

_____

_____

_____

Moses was strong enough to accept help because he knew it was for the greater outcome. How can you put this same strength of character into practice in your daily life?

_____

_____

_____

Chapter 2:

FEAR OF BEING ALONE

Teens Talk

Catie (15) shares her fear:

"I'm sort of embarrassed to admit this, but I am afraid of being alone. I am 15 years old, and both my parents work and don't get home until 6 pm every night.

"I have to come home from school by myself every day. I've done it for a couple of years now, but I still hate it as much as the first day. When I come in, I lock all the doors behind me, and turn the tv down really low so I can hear if anyone tries to break in. I never answer the phone unless I hear my folks leaving a message, and there's NO WAY I ever answer the door.

"I call my mom as soon as I walk in and if I hear anything weird, I call her back. I don't like being alone.

"It's worse in the winter months because it gets dark about an hour before they get home. I turn on all the lights, inside and outside, until they get home.

"I haven't told them how I feel, but I'm sure they've got to know. I'm hoping it will just go away one day. But it's already been two years. There are lots of other kids that go home alone, but I think I'm the only one who feels scared."

Sara (15) responds:

"I've been comin' home alone from school for 3 years. It's never been one of my favorite things, but I'm not afraid like I used to be. As soon as I walked into the house, I would check every closet, look under every bed . . . the whole nine yards.

"One day a girl from down the street knocked on my door because she'd heard a noise in her house that scared her. So she came to my house. We both talked about how we were afraid to go home alone everyday. I had no idea that anyone else felt that way. I was so relieved to know that I wasn't just crazy.

"We decided to stick together — one day she would come to my house, the next day I would go and stay with her. We did this for close to 2 years until she moved away.

"Now I'm back to coming home alone, but I see things totally different than I used to. I know that I'll be ok.

Maybe you could find a friend to come to your house with you. You're not the only one feeling the way you feel. No one likes being alone.

"If you can't find a friend to come stay with you, then call a friend. You could study together over the phone, or just have girl talk. The time will fly by, and your parents will be home before you realize it."

Brea (14) shares her fear:

"I am afraid of being alone, I know it's stupid, but every night when I go to bed, I lay in bed so scared that I cry all

night. I'm afraid of the dark, and I leave a light on in my bedroom, but my parents yell at me to turn it off. I can't tell them I'm scared.

"I wish I could go to sleep before 2 or 3 am, but I hear every little noise and imagine all sorts of horrible things."

Ashley (15) responds:

"I used to be afraid when I went to bed at night. Sometimes I'd pull the covers almost completely over my head, except for my nose and eyes, so I could breathe. I would lie facing my window so I could see if anyone came up to it. I'd be dripping with sweat, but it didn't stop me from lying there all covered up.

"Then, I realized that I was letting fear run my life. There was never anyone at my window. And covering my head never did any good at all. I decided to do something about it. I turned on my favorite radio station and let the music soothe me to sleep. I also began praying every night and I asked God to protect me and my family. And you know what? He always has.

"So, now I go to bed without any fear. Maybe you could start a bedtime "ritual" of some sort — you know, with things that make you comfortable. Maybe read from a good book, or hold on to a stuffed teddy bear. And I'll bet if you prayed for God to take away your fear and help you fall asleep quickly, He will do it. And maybe you won't be afraid anymore, just like me."

Scott (15) responds:

"Most of the kids at school see me as a pretty cool guy, but they don't know that I'm afraid to go to sleep at night. My brother rags on me all the time because I fall asleep with my light on and get freaky if I wake up and it's dark.

Forget the teddy bear, I'd rather sleep with a baseball bat by my pillow. Seriously, I have started trying to get a grip on why I'm so freaked out when the lights go out.

"One thing that has helped me is to have a night light turned on in the bathroom across the hall from my bedroom. And I've started praying every night while I'm laying there trying to sleep. I figure if something bad is gonna happen, it most likely won't happen while I'm praying. Sounds kinda dumb, but it's actually been helping me some."

Tracie (19) responds:

"Nothing is worse than being afraid to go to sleep. That's when you're supposed to be the most relaxed. I think anyone who laughs at you for being afraid is pretty insensitive. You should talk to your folks and tell them how you feel.

"I think praying is a brilliant idea, nothing dumb about that at all! Whatever works!"

Kim (19) shares her fear:

"I have to drive home late at night by myself every weekend from school. I finish up work around 10, and then I've got a two hour drive home.

"I keep thinking someone's following me, or I worry about having a flat tire or being stranded on the side of the road.

"I want to come home on weekends to see my family and my boyfriend. But I hate the late drive by myself. I make myself sick worrying about it every Friday. Anyone else ever feel this way, or am I the only idiot who's afraid to drive alone at night?"

Alexandria (19) responds:

"It's normal for a girl to be afraid on the road at midnight by herself, but I don't think it's particularly smart or safe if you've got a choice. I mean, couldn't you go home from work, get to bed immediately, and leave early, like at 7 am, and be home by breakfast?

"If you insist on going home late at night, be smart and get a cell phone. Call home when you leave work, and let your folks know the route you're taking. Have them be on the lookout for you. The cell phone would be great for calling 911 if you have car trouble, too.

"And I always have some pepper spray or mace on my key chain. I've never had to use it, but it gives a little peace of mind.

"I think that sometimes we need to completely avoid dangerous situations (like choosing to drive late at night when there's the option of the next morning), instead of tempting fate. I don't think we should live in fear, but sometimes we have to use our brain and make smart choices."

John (17) shares his fear:

"I work at a convenience store during the week after school to earn some extra money. I also work on the weekends. My job is ok, but I hate it when I have to work late and close. I'm usually the only one working that shift, and it's not on the best side of town.

"I don't know what I'd do if something were to happen. I just know I'd freak out if someone tried to rob me. I don't want to think about it, but I do. All the time. My mom worries about me, too. And I feel like such a wimp for being afraid. I just think I'd feel a little better if someone were there with me."

Justin (18) responds:

"Man, I know what you mean. I used to work at a video store late on the weekends, and I'd have to close and handle all the cash. There were windows all around, and I always felt like I was being watched when I closed the register.

"I used to lock the door and make a mad dash for my car every night. It was crazy. I finally told my boss that he either needed to have someone else there with me to close, or change my schedule. I didn't want to work the closing shift anymore. That was not a cool gig. Unfortunately, he couldn't afford to pay two people to work, and that was the time he needed me, so I lost my job. But y'know what? I found another one. And it was one where I could work in the afternoons, and I didn't have to be alone."

Kim (17) responds:

"There is no way I'd work a job where I was afraid. Is minimum wage really worth all that? No way. I say, find a new job. You'll be happier, and so will your mom."

Sandra (17) responds:

"If you really like (and need) your job, and you just don't like being alone, pray that God will protect you. Ask God for his divine protection and have the faith to believe that He will keep you safe. And ask Him to help you have the faith to believe if it's a little tough at first.

"Sometimes you can't just walk away from something, like a job, if you really need it. You have to follow your gut instinct, and pray."

What The Bible Has To Say

We all have nights when we are unable to fall asleep. But fear should never be one of the reasons. We read in Proverbs 3:24 that *"you can lie down without fear and enjoy pleasant dreams."*

We all have times when we are alone, and while we need to use wisdom in safety, we do not have to live in fear.

God wants us to feel His protection around us at all times. 1 Peter 3:12 *"The eyes of the Lord watch over those who do right, and his ears are open to their prayers ..."* That should encourage us to make prayer a priority in our lives.

Proverbs 1:33 says, *"But all who listen to me will live in peace and safety, unafraid of harm."*

Here's something very comforting: God is faithful to keep His promises. *"Understand, therefore, that the LORD your God is indeed God. He is the faithful God who keeps his covenant for a thousand generations and constantly loves those who love him and obey his commands.* (Deuteronomy 7:9)

This means we can always trust that God will be with us, looking after us, and loving us. . . keeping the promises He has made, like all the scriptures which promise His protection. As long as we serve God, He will keep us safe from all harm.

Here is another encouraging scripture, found in Isaiah, 41:13. It quotes the Lord, *"I am holding you by your right hand – I, the Lord your God. And I say to you, 'Do not be afraid, I am here to help you."*

Psalms 46:1 says, *"God is our refuge and strength, always ready to help in times of trouble.*

If God be for us, WHO can be against us??? (Romans 8:31) We can take good comfort in that!

How Does This Apply To Me?

When you're alone and feel frightened, what exactly are you afraid of? Can you name it?

_____

_____

_____

If God is faithful to keep His promises, which of His promises will help you overcome your fear of being alone?

_____

_____

_____

Do you spend time every day talking to God? How would it help you to trust Him if you spent more time talking to Him?

_____

_____

_____

Chapter 3:

FEAR OF BEING "THE NEW KID"

Teens Talk

Jason (15) shares his fear:

"I'm 15 and this year I'm going to a new school cuz my dad had to transfer to another city. I'm shy and quiet, and people are mistaking me for being stuck up. I miss my old friends. It's been about a month now, and I'm afraid I will never have any friends here. I'm scared that I'll never fit in.

"I can't tell my parents because my dad already feels bad about making us move. I don't want him to feel guilty."

Jamie (15) responds:

"I think one of the worst things for teens is thinking that we can't talk to our parents. I felt the same way when we had to move last year. Dad's boss said he had to transfer to another state or be laid off. It wasn't like we had a whole lot

of choice, but it sure did make me upset.

"I cried for weeks. Dad had to commute and was only home every other weekend. It was horrible. Mom was irritable, my sisters and I were arguing all the time, and we knew once we finished out the school year, we were moving and leaving everything and everyone we loved.

"Dad understood and was really cool about it. He called a family meeting and let us tell him (and mom) everything we were feeling. It didn't change anything because we had to move, but at least we got to tell them how we felt.

"Then dad did something really cool. He told us that when we moved to the new house, he was buying a computer and we could email our friends back home every day. He also gave us phone cards to call our friends.

"It still wasn't a good thing when it came to moving, but it did make it easier knowing we could keep in touch with our good friends.

"We found a really good church with a great youth program and the kids there made us feel really welcome. Some of those same kids were in our new school, and that made it easier because it was like we had built-in friends.

"Church is a really good place to make friends. I don't think it would have been nearly as easy on us if mom and dad hadn't found a church that cares about kids."

Shaundra (15) shares her fear:

"I am making the transition from being home schooled to public school this year and I'm scared to death! Mom and dad said it's my choice, so I'm not being forced to do something I don't want to do.

"The thing is, most of my church friends go to the public school, and they have so many more opportunities to do fun things. They're always talking about school parties and ball games, and just sitting around at lunch together. I feel

like I'm really missing out on a lot by staying home.

"I would like to talk to someone else who made the transition just to see how they did it."

Lucas (17) responds:

"I was home schooled until I was 13, and then I decided to go into public school. I know how you feel. There's excitement, but anxiousness. I couldn't wait to go my first day, and I dreaded it, all at the same time.

"I think the scariest part was not knowing what to expect. For the most part, it was a lot like going to youth events at church, only without the religious emphasis.

"Fortunately for you, you already know some of the kids and they're your friends. That should make it a lot better and friendlier from the start. Just remember that making friends is a two-way street."

Tara (16) responds:

"I switched over to public school last year from being home schooled, but it wasn't my choice. Mom had to go back to work because dad got laid off from the airlines. It was not a happy time for us at home, but I tried to be positive about it.

"Turned out to be one of the best things I've ever done. I liked being home schooled because I had a lot more free time during the day than I do now in school. But I have tons more friends. I'm also playing in the marching band, which I could never have done at home.

"I'm glad things worked out so good for me. It took a lot of pressure off my mom, and I think it helped her not to feel so guilty."

Owen (14) shares his fear:

"Kids can be really mean! We moved right after the school year and I have to start a new school. I feel sick to my stomach thinking about it.

"I'm not outgoing, and I'm not a cool, good looking guy. I don't wanna be singled out and laughed at. I just wanna make a few friends and have everyone else leave me alone. How can I make friends with people I don't even know?"

Joshua (16) responds:

"I haven't ever had to change schools, but my best friend moved here two years ago and he was the new kid for a while.

*"The **new kid** isn't necessarily the only one afraid to go to school, or wanting to make friends. I am very quiet and shy. Before Jax came to our school, I didn't have any good friends. There were a few people I talked to, but no one that I really called a friend.*

"Jax is very outgoing and he's friendly to everyone. He found out that I build remote-control airplanes and he was fascinated. He came home with me after school one day to fly planes, and we've been best friends ever since.

"He has lots of friends at school and I don't think the first day was a big deal to him. I was the one who was lonely.

"So, remember that someone else could be looking for a friend too!"

Kiesha (15) shares her fear:

"I decided to try out for the cheerleading squad this year. I was a cheerleader in junior high, but this was varsity. Pretty major.

"I was thrilled when I made it, but now I'm the only new

member to the squad. It wouldn't be so bad, but all the girls already know each other. They already have routines that they learned together last year. I'm really struggling trying to learn all the cheers and routines, and they have it all together. I feel like such an outsider. I wanted this to be fun, but so far it's just been horrible!"*

Christina (17) responds:

"I admire you for making the varsity squad. I have always wanted to try out, but I'm too much of a klutz.

"Have you tried talking to the captain? Maybe you could meet with her, one on one, and ask if she'd help you. Tell her you want the squad to be the best they can be, and if you are unsure of your steps, that could be a problem. If she's a good captain, she should be willing to work a little harder with you."

John (17) responds:

*"This is sorta out of my area . . . but maybe you could come up with a dance routine of your own, something really creative, and present it to the squad. Then **you** could teach **them** something new. If it's a great routine, I bet they'd be excited to learn it, and you'd be part of the gang."*

What The Bible Has To Say

You may have heard it said that the best way to make a friend is to first **be a friend**. It's true. The Bible tells us over and over again about loving one another, and the benefits from doing so.

Look at this scripture from Proverbs 3 (verses 3-4):

"Never let loyalty and kindness get away from you! Wear them like a necklace; write them deep within your heart. Then you will find favor with both God and people, and you will gain a good reputation."

Being the "new kid" in a completely new environment can be frightening. But it can also be exciting. Sometimes we make the mistake of thinking we have to **replace** friends. The truth is we can never have **too many friends!**

Look at this new experience as an opportunity to add new people to your **circle of friends.** You can look forward to special occasions, like Christmas. Just think how much fun it would be to send out Christmas e-cards or to hand make your own cards and mail them to all your friends . . . then wait on the return mail!

Here's the secret: When you **act** like a friend, almost always you will **receive** friendship in return. Don't be reactive. Don't **wait** on someone else to be the friend first. Be pro-active. Take the first step! Be brave.

And always be kind to people. Be honest and trustworthy. When you befriend someone and treat them with loyalty and genuine kindness, your friendship will be returned.

How Does This Apply To Me?

What is your description of a *friend*?

_____

_____

_____

Have you been friendly and made an effort to start a conversation with anyone in your new surroundings? What have you done?

_____

_____

_____

What are some things you can do to be pro-active in befriending people?

_____

_____

_____

If your goal is to form one or two new, strong friendships, what can you do to achieve that goal?

_____

_____

_____

What acts of kindness have you done recently?

_____

_____

_____

How do you respond when someone treats you kindly or attempts to befriend you?

_____

_____

_____

Chapter 4:

FEAR OF CHANGE

Teens Talk

Merry (16) shares her fear:

"I'm 16 years old, and my mom is getting married again. (My parents divorced four years ago.) The guy she's marrying is ok, but I'm afraid things will change after they get married.

"I wish things could stay the same. It makes me mad that everyone else is affecting my life and I have no say in the matter. I'm afraid I won't ever be in control of my life."

Otto (18) responds:

"My parents divorced several years ago. I had a hard time coping with not having my dad around every day. We are very close, so it was difficult for me to only get to see him every other weekend.

"After a while, my mom started to date. That was really

weird, and I didn't like it at all! I felt like it was a betrayal
to my dad, and to me. She met a guy that she dated for
about a year and they got married two years ago. I have to
say that I was angry at first. But I did like this guy, and he
treated me good.

"My mom said if I wanted to be happy living in the same
house as him, I needed to give him a chance. At first I felt
guilty, like I was betraying my dad. But I got really tired of
always being angry. I figured it wouldn't hurt to try.

"I prayed for God to give me an open mind and help me
get over my fear of change. It wasn't easy, but I did eventually begin to see a change in the relationship with my step-
dad. We began to grow closer, and we are actually okay
friends now.

"He will never take my dad's place, and he wasn't trying to. God helped me to realize that just because things
change, it doesn't mean it has to be for the worse. God can
take a bad situation and make it into a good thing if you
trust Him."

Frank (17) shares his fear:

"Change frightens me. I hate having to do new things.
Like a new school year terrifies me. I hate new classrooms,
new courses, and especially the thought of college next year.

"I hate everything about change — it has always made
me nervous. I don't even like the change of seasons. I get in
my comfort zone, and if anything challenges that, I cringe,
and fight it every step of the way. But things change anyway.
There's nothing I can do about it. So, I know somehow I've
got to manage this fear.

"I don't attempt new challenges, I want to try to keep
everything in my life the same. I know that if anything devastating were to ever happen, I would freak. I don't know
how I would handle it. I know this sounds weird. It feels

weird to even write about it. I'm not crazy, but I know this isn't normal. What can I do?"

Daniel (19) responds:

"Change can be scary — probably because it's different from what we're used to. But all change isn't bad. Some are actually kinda fun and exciting.

"I want things to stay the same, too. I feel safe if nothing ever changes. But that's not the way life is. In the real world, things change — sometimes daily. Not only did my parents divorce, but as soon as my mom remarried, we moved to a new state. I had to change schools my senior year in high school. Talk about a bummer! I had to leave my friends I had known for years, and wanted to graduate with — for a whole new family, home, and school. It was terrible.

"I was angry all the time and I took it out on the people I love the most. I was determined not to make new friends, and I was only making myself more miserable by the minute. Finally, one of my new teachers sat me down and told me that if I didn't get a better attitude and pull my grades up, I would flunk and wouldn't graduate.

"Man, I just about wigged out! She said she'd get me hooked up in some clubs on campus and introduce me to classmates I had a lot in common with. She really helped change my whole attitude. Mostly she just shook me up to see how stupid I was being, ruining the best part of my life.

"I got a grip and started pulling my grades up, and started making new friends. I made a point to tell this teacher how thankful I was that she'd been straight up with me. She told me that she'd been praying for me, and that God showed her how to help me.

"That was over the top, man. I couldn't believe God cared that much for me!

"Just a few weeks ago I asked God into my heart, with my

favorite teacher by my side. I haven't worried so much about change lately because I know that God will see me through any situation, and it might even be a great new experience."

Jackie (17) shares her fear:

"I'm 17 and it's time to be doing all the stuff to plan for college.But I can't make up my mind about where I want to apply, or what I want to do with my life.

"It's really weird, but I think more than being afraid of change, I'm actually afraid of making a decision. I want to keep all my options open, so I put off making a decision, sometimes until it's too late. I wonder if I'll ever be able to deal with change, or with making a decision."

Gil (17) responds:

"I don't think that sounds weird at all. Most of my friends are having trouble deciding things like where to go to college, where to work, whether to even go to college — all the stuff we have to think about now that graduation is near.

"I'm kinda looking forward to the changes, but at the same time, I'm afraid that if I choose plan A, I'll regret it and wish I'd chosen Plan B. I'm having difficulty getting perspective and feeling good about making a decision.

"A good friend of mine is into making lists. She divides a paper into two columns and writes down all the pros and cons to a situation. She says seeing it in black and white helps her to come to grips with what's the best choice.

"It sounds like something that might work for both of us!"

What The Bible Has To Say

Change is the essence of the world. It's ironic that the only consistent thing **is** change.

To fear change means living under the bondage of fear, every hour of every day. You can't escape change — but you can escape the fear of change.

Imagine if Moses had allowed fear to rule his life. Would the Israelites have remained slaves to Egypt? Would they have ever reached the promised land? How much of history would have been changed if Moses had given in to the power of fear?

Many times the root of this fear is being confused about the situation and circumstances around us, and not knowing which direction to go. James 1:5 says *"If you need wisdom – if you want to know what God wants you to do – ask him, and he will gladly tell you."* God will guide your steps each and every day. And with His guidance, there is nothing to fear.

If you are experiencing the fear of change, then you need to know that you have authority **through the name of Jesus Christ** to tell that fear to leave you.

Yes, that's right, speak to it directly. Bind that spirit of fear in the name of Jesus. Why? Because fear is not of God. *"For God has not given us the spirit of fear and timidity, but of power, love, and a sound mind."* II Timothy 1:7.

I Corinthians 14:33 tells us that *"God is not a God of disorder, but of peace...."* Therefore, we know that anything other than peace should have no place in a Christian's life.

How Does This Apply To Me?

What was the last change you had to face? Describe it in detail.

_____

_____

_____

How did you feel about this change?

_____

_____

_____

How did you deal with it — did you resist, or did you try to adapt?

_____

_____

_____

If God says that you can ask Him for wisdom and He will give it to you, do you believe that includes the wisdom to accept and handle changes?

_____

_____

_____

Since the Bible tells us God has not given us the spirit of fear, do you think He wants you to turn to Him, trust Him and let go of the fear?

_____

_____

_____

How do you think you can do that?

_____

_____

_____

Chapter 5:

FEAR OF CRITICISM

Teens Talk

Dustin (15) shares his fear:

"I hate criticism. Sometimes I won't even start a project at school because I'm afraid that my teachers and classmates will criticize my work.

"Like last year, I wrote an essay about politics and read it in class. The teacher picked it apart and told me everything that was wrong with it. I guess I should learn something from that, but I don't know how to find anything positive in criticism. I just shut down whenever someone starts to tell me what I've done wrong and what I should have done."

Dave (16) responds:

"Man, been there, done that! But let me tell you, shutting down is the worst kind of defeat. You know why?

Because there's no hope in achieving anything when you shut down.

"The scary part of criticism is that you open yourself up and become vulnerable. I remember what that was like when I auditioned for our church youth praise team. It was the scariest thing I'd ever done.

"The first time I auditioned, I didn't make it. The director was nice, he explained to me why I wasn't chosen, and what I could do to improve my voice. I guess I could have gotten really mad and stomped away to never sing again, and it did hurt, but I decided to take his advice.

"I practiced for hours, and when they had auditions again the next year, I had a lot more confidence. I used the criticism to my advantage. Yes, I was still afraid, but the biggest thing I learned was that I didn't have to let fear shut me down. I learned how to believe in myself. I think that even if I had been turned down, the experience would have been worth it because I didn't let fear get the best of me. That's a good feeling!

"And my mom never stopped telling me that some of the most successful people in the world have been turned down many times before they made it."

Ben (16) shares his fear:

"Man, I don't want nobody telling me what to do or how to do it. I'm 16 and I'm no kid. No one knows better than me how I feel, and they don't know if I've done my best or not. I mean, it is embarrassing and humiliating when someone tries to act like you've done everything all wrong. I don't like being embarrassed!"

Shari (16) responds:

"Whoa, you need to chill, Ben! First of all, even when

you've done your best, there's always room for improve-
ment. Maybe the person giving you criticism is doing it all
wrong, but that's no excuse for acting like you know it all
when you don't.

"Don't get me wrong, I'm not judging you. There's just
no way that any 16 year old can know everything. That'd be
a good lesson for you to learn now."

Marty (19) responds:

"Nobody likes criticism. We all think we're good at
everything we do, but we aren't. That's why we need people
to give us advice on how to be better. Sometimes that means
hearing things we don't wanna hear if it'll make us better in
the long run.

"For example, I took a business class my senior year in
high school. Part of the class was how to have a successful
job interview. Every student had to sit down **one on one** with
the teacher and pretend she was an employer interviewing
us. She asked all kinds of questions, and I stunk. I didn't
know how to sell myself, and the one and only question I
asked her was how much the job paid — **a real big no-no.**

"She was really critical and told me (in front of the
class) all the things I did wrong. I was so angry and embarrassed in front of my classmates. But later that year I had my
first real job interview, and they asked me some of the same
questions she had asked in class. I was prepared, and I even
got the job!

"So, even though you may not like being criticized, first,
consider the source. What's their intention? Is it to help
you? Do they know what they're talking about?

"If they have your best interest at heart, listen to what
they have to say. Apply what you think you should, and store
the rest in a "brain file" for another time you may need it."

Ashley (15) responds:

*"The key word here is **corrective** criticism. It's still not easy to hear when someone is critiquing you, but if they do it in the right way, it's meant to help you, not hurt you. It might sting when you hear it, but it will help when you need it. Make sense?"*

Cooper (17) shares his fear:

"I recently decided to graduate from the church youth choir to the adult choir. I know it's going to be a lot more challenging for me, and I just found out that I have to audition.

"This bums me out. I've heard that the auditions are tough. There's 3 judges, I guess you'd call them. They audition for natural vocal ability, but they will also make me sight read a song I've never seen before. I'll be tested on tonal memory, and then they have some questions about my Christian life. And it's all video taped.

"I'm horrified at the thought. I'm not a great sight reader, and I've heard the atmosphere is like majorly tense, and they give you a critique immediately afterwards.

"I've thought about backing out. I mean, what if I don't make it? That would be so embarrassing. I want to do it so bad, but I don't think I can handle them telling me all the bad things I did in my audition. Maybe God is just trying to tell me something."

Carol (17) responds:

"First of all, God doesn't give us fear to teach us a lesson. The Bible tells us there is no fear in Him. I mean, every where you look in the Bible you see 'Fear not...Fear not....Fear not...' So why would He then turn around and

use fear to teach us something? He wouldn't. So, just get rid of that thought. Sorry, but that was stupid.

"Next, don't let anybody at church intimidate you. If you are wanting to sing for God, then do it. He will help you do your best, and if it's not good enough for the adult choir, then go back to the youth choir for a year until you can work on developing your voice or sight reading some more.

"Listen to what they tell you. I don't think they'd criticize you to be mean, but they will be giving you suggestions to help you sing better. I mean, shouldn't we do our best and be at our best if we are going to do it for God?"

Leroy (18) responds:

"Keep your head clear, man. Don't let a bunch of crud floating around in your brain keep you from auditioning. We all can learn from criticism, if it's done in a professional way. Don't give up on a dream you have just because you're afraid of what someone may or may not say. That's so not cool."

What The Bible Has To Say

The ego can be easily bruised sometimes, but an inflated ego and refusing to accept corrective criticism (whether it's by fear or arrogance) is totally self-defeating.

The Bible speaks very plainly about people who refuse to accept criticism (instruction or correction). Proverbs 10:8 says that *"the wise are glad to be instructed, but babbling fools fall flat on their faces."*

Whoa! Imagine calling someone a *babbling fool* and living to tell about it! And yet, here it is.

In the same chapter, verse 17, it says that *"people who accept correction are on the pathway to life. . ."* If you believe that scripture, then wouldn't it stand to reason that someone who **will not take** correction from those qualified to give it, is walking into defeat and destruction?

While we're at it, let's just cut to the chase here. Is it stupid to ignore someone who is giving you correction and criticism? You bet it is. Proverbs 12:1 says *"to learn, you must love discipline; it is stupid to hate correction."*

In order for us to be the wise Christians God wants us to be, we must be strong enough to withstand constructive criticism.

Please understand that we **do not** and **should not** take any type of physical abuse. We are talking about instruction or criticism which is done **in love and meant for our well being**. We are supposed to accept that kind of correction and use it constructively in our lives.

You can discern the difference between abuse and constructive criticism by the scripture verse Proverbs 12:18. It says, *"Some people make cutting remarks, but the words of the wise bring healing."* And Proverbs 10:32 says, *"The godly speak words that are helpful, but the wicked speak only what is corrupt."*

So, the bottom line is this: We need to be strong in

knowing who we are in Jesus Christ, and that *"we can do all things through Christ who strengthens us."*

If we know this, we can accept godly, wise criticism and apply it as needed. And we can take confidence in knowing that we are even more wise than before.

How Does This Apply To Me?

Proverbs 10:8 says that *"the wise are glad to be instructed, but babbling fools fall flat on their faces."* If you had to rewrite that about yourself, how would you say it?

_____

_____

_____

Proverbs 15:31-32 says: *"If you listen to constructive criticism, you will be at home among the wise. If you reject criticism, you only harm yourself; but if you listen to correction, you grow in understanding."* What does this mean to you?

_____

_____

_____

Proverbs 13:18 says, *"If you ignore criticism, you will end in poverty and disgrace; if you accept criticism, you will be honored."* Why do you think people who ignore criticism will end in poverty and disgrace?

_____

_____

_____

If continuing to be angered by or fearful of criticism will bring you poverty and disgrace, would you want to change your behavior?

_____

_____

_____

How do you think you can change your behavior?

_____

_____

_____

What do you think the Bible means by *" if you accept criticism, you will be honored"?*

_____

_____

_____

If *"the words of the wise bring healing,"* how can you begin to accept corrective criticism in a positive manner?

_____

_____

_____

Chapter 6:

FEAR OF DIVORCE

Teens Talk

Garret (14) shares his fear:

"I am 14 years old, and I am depressed all the time. My parents divorced four years ago, and I can't seem to get past it.

"They argued all the time, so at least now there is some peace in the house. But I want to have my dad around. I miss seeing him at the end of the day and playing ball and stuff like that. Now I only see him every other weekend.

I just wish my parents could work things out and get back together. I think about it all the time, but, after this long, I don't think it'll ever happen.

"I can't concentrate on my schoolwork, and I don't have fun with my friends. I wonder if I could've done something to prevent their divorce. I try to be good.

Do all kids of divorced parents feel this way? Or is there something wrong with me?"

Grace (17) responds:

"Kids of divorce feel all kinds of rotten things. Trust me, I know. My folks divorced when I was 14. I spent a whole year wishing and praying that they would get back together.

"I got mad at God for not making them get back together . . . I kept thinking 'He's God, he can do anything.'

"I don't want to sound all preachy, but the truth is God won't make us do anything. My mom and dad have minds of their own, and it's up to them to make their own choices. So now I'm trying to let go of the past and move into the present.

"I still am not happy about my parents' divorce, but I know that it's not God's fault, or my fault. I still love both my parents, and I know they love me. That's really the most important thing. Everything else is just junk that can be worked around."

Chad (15) responds:

"My folks divorced two years ago. I was 13. I don't know if they stopped to think about how my brother and I would feel when they divorced. But things got a lot worse before they got better. It was kinda like my dad died because he left the house and we rarely saw him. Mom didn't talk about him, and it was like he just disappeared.

"I was scared to talk about him too much, or cry cause I missed him. I didn't think mom wanted me to love him anymore. My brother dropped out of school and everything.

"About a year after my dad moved out, mom decided to talk to our pastor about my brother and me because things just weren't getting any better. He said we needed Christian counseling, man that stank! I didn't want to talk to a stranger about our private stuff. But I went cause mom made me.

"But I think the counseling was a good thing cause mom found out how we felt, and that we still needed both parents.

She didn't know how the whole thing had made us feel. I don't know HOW she didn't know, I mean we went from having a dad around all the time, to him being completely gone. Duh!

"Anyway, mom talked to dad about going to the same counselor, and he did. The counselor suggested something really weird — a family session with both my mom, dad, and us.

"It ended up being a really cool thing. Mom and dad explained things that we'd never talked about, like my brother and I didn't cause the divorce. And we got to talk about how we loved dad and mom and didn't want to take sides. For the first time I think mom and dad saw how me and my brother felt.

"We're doing much better now because we talk about our feelings. It helps to just get it out there in the open."

Isaac (14) responds:

"My parents aren't divorced, but my best friend's parents are. He's going through a really hard time now. He was afraid that all his friends would dump him and stop hangin' with him.

"I don't know why he'd think that, but it made me work harder to be a better friend. Sometimes we don't know the right things to say to a friend, but my advice would be to let them know you're there, and to just listen if you can't do anything else."

Carly (19) shares her fear:

"I've been going out with the same guy for 3 years now. He keeps saying that we'll be together forever. He gave me a promise ring, and told me that the ring is a promise that he will marry me once we graduate college.

"I accepted the ring, but I'm really afraid that I did the

wrong thing. I am a child of divorced parents. Their marriage was awful, and the divorce was even worse. If that's what marriage is all about, they can have it!

"I don't know what went wrong with them. My brother and I were miserable all the time. I can't stand the thought of going through what my parents did. And I wouldn't ever want to do that to my children.

"So, even though I love my boyfriend, I don't think I want to get into marriage — it might end in divorce one day."

Ling Chu (20) responds:

"Is there any reason why you think it would end in divorce? If there's a legitimate reason, then duh, yeah, you need to split with this guy now. I mean, if he's got habits that drive you nuts now, it'll only be worse after 5-10 years.

"But if you love him in spite of those habits, and you think you can live with them, then don't fear something that will probably never happen. And you can't make your decision based on your parents' history.

"Besides, you still have college to go through. You will probably have a totally different outlook on things after that. My point is that you don't need to be worried about it right now. Take one day at a time, and enjoy the relationship as it is now. God will help you make the decision about marriage when the time comes."

Alysha (19) responds:

"Girl, let me tell you, just because your parents had a rough time of it doesn't mean you're gonna follow in their footsteps.

"You just need to be sure you know your guy very well. Pay attention to the small things, and communicate with him. Guys don't really like to talk, but it's very important.

"I've been praying for my perfect mate for years. I've asked God to pick out the right guy for me. And I've prayed that God will help him to be the spiritual leader he should be. I believe that God has that perfect spouse for me and that He is preparing him just for me. Maybe you should begin to pray that as well. That will give you a peace about things I'm sure. It really helped me.

"And with God in control and allowing Him to bring that person into your life, whether it's your current boyfriend or not, you won't have to be preoccupied with divorce right now. Make up your mind that when you say yes, you are making a lifelong commitment. Don't even let divorce be a thought in your mind."

Geena (19) responds:

"You are TOO young to know who you want to spend the rest of your life with! You need to just relax and have some fun and enjoy life now. If you're having doubts, then don't make ANY decision. Just be honest with the guy, don't lead him on. That's just cheap!

"But divorce isn't hereditary. (Ain't that prolific??) Just because your parents divorced, doesn't mean that you will. I think you just don't feel ready to commit and you're using your parent's divorce as a scape goat. But what do I know?"

What The Bible Has To Say

Sometimes things happen that are completely out of our control. And unfortunately, for a child, divorce is one of those things. A child doesn't cause it, and a child can't prevent it.

There are so many feelings that are associated with the process of divorce: guilt, anger, sadness, frustration, fear, helplessness, confusion. Divorce can affect every part of your life — it's your family, after all.

But there is good news. We have a Heavenly Father who loves us more than we can ever imagine, and His love for us never changes.

There is nothing we could ever do to make Him love us any more, or any less. He's the same yesterday, today and forever. And He wants to help us when we hurt, and He wants to take away the fear of what may lie ahead.

Phillipians 4:6-7 says:

"Don't worry about anything; instead, pray about everything. Tell God what you need, and thank Him for all He has done. If you do this, you will experience God's peace, which is more wonderful than the human mind can understand. His peace will guard your hearts and minds as you live in Jesus Christ."

Thank You Jesus! He is such a loving, kind and good God! He says that we just need to pray and give our fears to Him, and He will give us His peace in return.

We don't mean to make it sound easy, because the words *"don't worry about anything"* is a **very difficult thing to do**. Just remember — God is faithful and true to His Word. If we will trust Him, He will give us peace and He will take care of us.

And remember that ***"He heals the brokenhearted, binding up their wounds."*** (Psalm 147:3) There are a lot of wounds when parents divorce. There is a lot of healing that needs to take place. No, it won't happen overnight, but God will heal your hurt and see you through terrible ordeals such as divorce.

And His loving arms are always around you.

How Does This Apply To Me?

Psalms 71:5 says: ***"O Lord, You alone are my hope. I've trusted You, O Lord, from childhood."***

David said these words to his heavenly Father, and it offers us the promise that God is OUR hope. Write your own prayer below and say it every night:

_____

_____

_____

_____

_____

_____

Chapter 7:

FEAR OF EMBARRASSMENT

Teens Talk

Mike (15) shares his fear:

"I always feel embarrassed. I hate it when my parents talk about me in front of other people, even if it's just family. I hate people looking at me. I don't want any attention drawn to me. I just wanna blend in the crowd.

"I don't know why I feel this way. It makes no sense. And I don't necessarily like feeling this way, I'd like to not feel so self-conscious."

Jacob (18) responds:

*"I was the **KING** of embarrassment. I earned that title. Here's the worst part (for me) about being embarrassed:*

- *I could never look people in the eyes.*
- *I hung my head down hoping no one would ever look at me.*
- *I never went to parties, and always avoided large crowds.*
- *I didn't want any attention on me at all.*
- *I could NEVER hide my embarrassment, it was like a stupid sign around my neck!*

"I don't know why I felt this way. My parents are pretty outgoing, and have lots of friends. I've just never wanted to **stick out***.*

"It got so bad that it affected my speech. I began to slur my words, and mumble so low that my parents would blow up and yell at me to speak up. I'd avoid family during the holidays because I was too embarrassed to talk to them.

"My best friend invited me to go to Vacation Bible School with him. He told me about all the cool things they did, and he made it sound like so much fun, I went. During one of the classes, the teacher began to talk about how Mary had loved Jesus so much, in spite of what other people in the room thought about her, she washed Jesus' feet, right there while people watched and made fun of her.

"He said that as Christians, we need to realize who we are through Jesus Christ. We need to be bold and strong.

"I had never been either of these. I knew I was a Christian, I just never looked at it that way before. **I __AM__ a child of God***.*

"I mean, I could almost instantly feel myself coming out of my shell. I felt a confidence that I'd never had before. I began, little by little, to overcome my fear of embarrassment. And whenever I would feel a sense of that fear, I would just remind myself of who I am in Christ."

Jules (14) shares her fear:

"I know exactly what you mean about being embar-rassed around family. I am taking vocal lessons and every time the family gets together for holidays, my mom is always making me sing for everyone.

"What really stinks is that I don't think anyone really wants to hear me sing anyway. They listen for a few seconds, then they all start talking again. It's awful!

"The last time we had a family party, I pretended to be sick and stayed in bed the whole time. I missed out on all the fun, too, but I just couldn't stomach singing again!

"I'm already worrying about the Christmas party. I should be looking forward to it, but I'm dreading it like crazy!"

Faith (18) responds:

"It's not fair that you have to entertain at all your fam-ily parties. Your mom probably just wants to show you off because she's proud of you. But that doesn't make it easier for you.

"I've never understood why kids don't at least take the risk of being honest with their parents. I mean, if you keep your mouth shut, you KNOW you've still got the problem. At least if you try to be honest with your mom, you stand a chance (no matter how remote) that you might find a way to solve it.

"Maybe a solution would be to tell your mom that you think it would be a great idea to have open Karaoke at ONE family party each year. That way everyone has an opportu-nity to sing (including you), but it's just once a year. That kinda makes it easier in two ways . . . 1. you're not alone in performing, and 2. you only have to dread it once a year.

"Just a thought, hope it works out!"

What The Bible Has To Say

There's a lady in the Bible who put herself in a position of great embarrassment simply because she wanted to show Jesus how much she loved Him.

Stop for a moment and read John 12:1-8.

Jesus was having dinner with his disciples in a friend's house. After dinner, Mary was overwhelmed with love for Jesus, and she wanted to show Him. She disappeared from the room, and came back with a very expensive bottle of perfume (possibly worth more than $25,000 today). She broke the bottle and poured the perfume all over Jesus' feet.

This won't sound like a big deal to you because our culture is SO different now, but back then it was shocking. Here's why:

1. Without a dowry, Mary had little to no chance of ever getting married. The perfume was her dowry, and it was worth a fortune.

2. Back then, an unmarried woman was worthless and pretty much unable to take care of herself financially. Mary was unmarried, and now that she had used her dowry, **she had completely sacrificed her whole life to show Jesus her love and devotion.**

3. In that day, women did not let their hair down in public. It was a tremendous breach in etiquette. Mary broke that etiquette so that she could wipe Jesus' feet.

Now imagine how the people in the room might have reacted to Mary's behavior. They probably gasped and were shocked, some might have smirked and laughed at her.

Jesus knew Mary's motives, and he told everyone to leave her alone. The bottom line was that Mary didn't care what anyone thought about her.

Mary's love for Jesus gave her confidence to do the right thing.

How Does This Apply To Me?

Describe how Mary might have felt when she walked into a room full of people and broke the bottle of perfume and poured it over Jesus' feet.

_____

_____

_____

Describe how Mary might have felt when she heard the other people in the room gasping in shock at her actions, and Judas' comment about her wasting the perfume.

_____

_____

_____

Why do you think Mary put herself in that position, risking embarrassment?

_____

_____

_____

How do you think Mary overcame those feelings and was able to do it anyway?

_____

_____

_____

What do you think could help you to deal with embarrassment and find the strength to overcome it?

_____

_____

_____

Chapter 8:

FEAR OF BEING INSIGNIFICANT

Teens Talk

Mitch (14) shares his fear:

"I am the third and youngest child in our family. My older brother is in college and my sister is 17. I am 14, and I'm still treated like a child.

"I have strong opinions about things but no one seems to care. Whatever I say goes in one ear and out the other. I don't feel like an important part of this family. Everyone is always in a hurry, and there's always so much to do.

" I want to just have some time alone with my parents, but there's always something more important than me. When will my time come? When will I be as important as my brother and sister, and my parents' friends? I'm a person, too, and I want to feel special. I want to feel like I matter to someone, especially my parents."

Jeremy (19) responds:

"I am the middle child in my family — I have an older and younger sister. I always felt like I had to figure things out for myself. I was the only boy, and I had to do things for both my sisters.

"I remember when my older sister left for college. I couldn't wait for her to be gone! I figured I'd get all the attention then. Instead, I had to cart my little sister to dance classes, to school in the morning, you name it. If I complained to my parents, they said I was being selfish.

"Eventually, I got so angry that I ended up saying things that I regretted and couldn't take back. I wish I had handled things differently. I should have tried to talk to my parents rationally. I think they would have listened to me if I hadn't acted like such a jerk about it all.

"We ended up going to counseling and things are much better now. My parents actually admitted that they had ignored me, even if they hadn't meant to. It really helped to hear them say they were sorry. They're making an effort, and so am I. It goes both ways. But it's a daily thing — working at getting along and being honest and respectful with each other."

Tony (15) shares his fear:

"I have been depressed for two years and it's getting worse. My brother is perfect at everything he does. He's better in sports, in school, better looking, you name it. He doesn't have to try at anything, and I try so hard it hurts, but I always end up second best.

"I'm a really good Christian, and everyone acts like if you're a Christian, you always feel happy and nothing is ever wrong. So, I always act happy and put on a smiley face, and try to make everyone else feel good. But I'm so sad

inside, I feel like dying. I'm afraid to let anyone know how I feel because they'll think I'm selfish and just want attention. I just want to feel like I matter."

Paul (16) responds:

"I'm a Christian too, and it's not that I'm always **happy**, but I do have an inner peace that helps me to have a positive outlook. I guess I appear to be always happy because of that.

"But just because you're a Christian doesn't mean that you won't get upset, or feel angry sometimes, or even be treated fairly all the time. I think the difference for Christians is that we have someone we can always go to for help.

"First, have you even talked to your parents honestly about how you feel? Show them the comments you made here if you need a way to open the conversation. It's not selfish to have feelings, or to want to feel important. It's selfish to keep all these feelings to yourself until it becomes an even bigger problem. It's selfish to assume that no one will care about you if you DO tell.

"Secondly, have you tried to find something special that you can claim as all your own? Like a talent, or hobby, or something that you can really get into? That would help you to feel special, it would give you a creative outlet, and it would give your parents something to talk with you about.

"And never forget, you are VERY important and significant to God. He even knows how many hairs are on your head."

Wes (15) shares his fear:

"I'm in an accelerated biology class at school, which means I'm pretty much the youngest one. The teacher just *recently told us we'd be divided up into groups of 4 or 5 to work on projects throughout the year.*

"I'm really nervous about this. I'm afraid that my group will dump my ideas out the window because I'm younger than them. I'm scared they're going to think I don't have a clue and that my opinions don't matter. I can see it now . . . I'll be just sitting there listening and waiting for them to tell me what to do. Opening my mouth is not an option, I'm sure they think I'm nobody!"

Dan (17) responds:

"Don't sell yourself short, you're in that class for a reason. You're a brainer. You know your stuff. And, believe me, as someone who isn't the smartest guy in the class, I love being paired up with a brainer.

"Truth is, I rely on that person to help pull me through the class. So, they're lucky to have you. You need to quit thinking you don't measure up just because of your age. It doesn't fly here. You need to speak up. I bet you'll be really surprised at how they will react to you. And I mean, it will be a good surprise."

Jewel (17) responds:

"Come on, man. I always hate being in groups with people who just sit back and do nothing. It's like they're riding on our hard work and ideas. That's how it will come across to these folks, too.

"You need to be vocal. It's only fair. Even if the group doesn't go with your idea, you might spark an idea in someone else. That's what being a part of a group is all about. Age has nothing to do with it. You have to be a team player.

"If you're smart enough to be in the class, you need to

be smart enough to act like it. Use the smarts God blessed you with and ask Him to help you express yourself in a way that people will listen."

What The Bible Has To Say

We all have a different opinion of what is **valuable**. A garage sale is a perfect example of this. One person skips over something he considers useless, while another person stumbles upon the same item and thinks he's found a treasure. It's all relative to how one thinks and what one treasures in the heart.

Let's do a little Bible study together and look at the story of a man who felt the same way many of you feel. (Judges 6 & 7)

The story takes place during a horrible time for the people of Israel and a young farmer named Gideon. They were being tortured and starved to death by a group of desert people called The Medianites. It was so bad for Gideon and his people that many of them ran for their lives and hid in caves. Gideon's own father became so bitter that he built an altar to the false god, Baal, and turned his back on God.

One day when Gideon was out working in the field, the Lord said to him, ***"Go with the strength you have and rescue Israel from the Midianites. I am sending you!"***

Imagine how shocked Gideon must have felt. He basically said, "Look, my family is the wimpiest, weakest family in the whole town, and I'm the puniest of them all!"

Gideon wasn't one of those huge warriors you see in movies like **"Gladiator."** He was just the son of a farmer, a young man who had a strong love for God. And even though he felt insignificant, he was a man who trusted God, and that makes a person VERY significant.

When you read the story of Gideon, you'll see that not only did he feel small and insignificant, but God cut Gideon's army from tens of thousands to only 300 soldiers. God wanted to teach Gideon that his power, significance and importance was **only** through God.

God gave Gideon the strength and the wisdom to defeat

the Midianites with only three hundred men because **Gideon put all his faith and trust in God**. And because of that, he was **very valuable** to God — and to all of Israel as it turns out.

We are all valuable if Jesus Christ is the Lord and Savior of our lives. We are God's children. Nothing can make us more valuable than that. Proverbs 3:5-8 says:

> *"Trust in the Lord with all your heart; do not depend on your own understanding. Seek His will in all you do, and He will direct your paths. Don't be impressed with your own wisdom. Instead, fear the Lord and turn your back on evil. Then you will gain renewed health and vitality."*

How Does This Apply To Me?

When God told Gideon that he was going to rescue Israel, how did Gideon respond?

_____

_____

_____

Read Judges 6:15 to consider this next question. When Gideon told the Lord that his clan was the weakest in the whole tribe, and that HE was the least in his whole family, what was he really saying?

_____

_____

_____

Have you ever felt like the least valuable person in your family? What similarities do you see between yourself and Gideon?

_____

_____

_____

Look at yourself as GOD sees you, and write a description.

_____

_____

_____

How can you begin to see yourself as God sees you — His child, very special, unique, and valuable to the Kingdom?

_____

_____

_____

If God can use Gideon, He can use you, too. How can you make yourself available to God?

_____

_____

_____

Chapter 9:

FEAR AFTER LOSING
A LOVED ONE

Teens Talk

Gary (17) shares his fear:

"My good friend died a while back in an accident. My faith in God was really shaken because of it. I can't tell my parents because they wouldn't understand how I could question the Lord. I feel completely alone and I don't know where to turn.

"Several of my friends have tried to tell me that God still loves me even though I was angry and blamed Him, but I don't know how to get back to my walk with Him after this."

Wendy (20) responds:

"My Grandpa and I were very close. We lived just around the corner from each other. When I was growing up,

I would walk to his house everyday, and we'd spend great time together. He was real good at working with wood, and one summer we made a bird house together. He let me help, and we would laugh and talk while we worked. He understood me like no one else did. Nobody loved me like he did.

"*I was devastated when his car was hit by a drunk driver — he was killed instantly. I was in shock at first. Then I blamed the drunk driver. But he was pretty much going to be a vegetable the rest of his life, so I didn't feel right staying angry at him. So I blamed God.*

"*I couldn't understand why this happened. Why my Grandpa, who would never hurt another living soul? He was a good man. He loved God. He did all the right things. And he was healthy. He could have lived so many more years.*

"*I quit praying, I quit reading my Bible, and I would have quit going to church if my parents would've let me.*

"*But I'm so glad they made me go, because during a service I heard a song that said God is a God of second chances. And I learned that it was not God's fault — well, I knew that all along, and I really wanted to be close to God again, but didn't feel worthy.*

"*The words to that song changed my life forever, It said:* **'You (God) stand with arms wide open and You call my name. With a heart full of forgiveness, You love me the same. And though I'm not deserving of a love so true, You're still there waiting when I run back to You.'** *He's the God of second chances.*"

Scott (18) shares his fear:

"*My best friend died in a car wreck last year. We had been to the movies and he'd dropped me off at home. They say he fell asleep at the wheel and lost control of the car.*

"*I don't think I will ever be able to forgive myself. If I had just kept him at the house longer, invited him in, done*

*anything to keep him there, he might not have had the wreck.
I could have even let him spend the night.*

*"The worst part of it all is that I spent months blaming
God. I can't even pray now and ask for help. Why would He
help me when I blamed Him for Rick's death?"*

Carie (19) responds:

*"I haven't had a terrible experience like that, but I can
only imagine how much hurt you must have felt, for such a
long time. But, if God loved us so much that He'd send Jesus
to die for our sins, don't you think one of those sins would
be blaming Him for Rick's death?*

*"I do. I think that God knows us so well, He knows we
aren't perfect. He's the one who's perfect, and that's why He
will forgive you. That, and because He loves you."*

Todd (17) responds:

*"God definitely is forgiving. He's there for you, man,
specifically for times like these. You've gotta ask God to forgive you for blaming Him, and ask Him to help you quit
blaming yourself. You couldn't have any way of knowing
that Rick was gonna fall asleep driving. You did nothing
wrong. It's just a terrible thing that happened.*

"But you need God now more than ever."

What The Bible Has To Say

There are so many emotions after a loved one is gone. And there are times when blame is placed on God for taking this precious person from our lives. Sometimes, due to circumstances, it seems as if there is no one else to blame, just this burning need to assign blame to someone.

The good news is that God understands and forgives. Not only will He forgive our anger towards Him, but He will help us through the grieving process.

Do you remember Peter, the apostle? Jesus once said to Peter, *"Now I say to you that you are Peter, and upon this rock I will build my church, and all the powers of hell will not conquer it. And I will give you the keys of the Kingdom of Heaven."*

Can you imagine being so close to Jesus and hearing Him say such wonderful things about you? Can you then imagine doing something so terrible that you believe He could never forgive you? Imagine doing something so horrendous that you feel ashamed to be in His presence.

Peter had a very close relationship with Jesus and had many personal conversations with him, like the one above. And yet Jesus knew that Peter would deny knowing him. In fact, during the last supper Jesus predicted it. Peter said there was no way he'd ever deny knowing Jesus, that he was ready to go to prison or to death with Him.

But when he was put to the test, he failed, miserably, just as Jesus had predicted. Imagine how Peter felt when Jesus' words came back to haunt him. Imagine the shame and guilt that he carried around with him during the time Jesus was crucified.

And yet, after Jesus resurrected, he appeared to Peter several times. Peter went on to spend the rest of his life preaching the gospel of Jesus Christ and leading thousands to the Lord.

God loves us, and wants us to feel His presence and love at all times, especially during times of hurt. He will heal our hurt, forgive us and forget all the things we might say against Him, if we only ask Him to.

Philippians 4:8-9 helps us to get through such situations. *"Fix your thoughts on what is true and honorable and right. Think about things that are pure and lovely and admirable. Think about things that are excellent and worthy of praise...and the God of peace will be with you."*

If we keep our eyes focused on Him, we will find ourselves in the healing process. *"Now the God of hope fill you with all joy and peace in believing, that you may abound in hope, through the power of the Holy Ghost."* Romans 15:13.

There is no need to fear. God's grace is so much greater than we can even imagine. And it extends to each of us. We can take comfort in that truth. His love can never be taken away from us.

How Does This Apply To Me?

Betrayal by a trusted, beloved friend is devastating. Yet, even though Jesus knew Peter would deny knowing him, Jesus said this about Peter:

> *"... Now I say to you that you are Peter, and upon this rock I will build my church ..."*

What does this tell you about Jesus' love?

_____

_____

_____

Spend some time in the New Testament and look at Peter's ministry after Jesus' ascension. What does his life say about the forgiveness and mercy of our heavenly Father?

_____

_____

_____

God's love for you is much greater than you can comprehend. Write your name in the blanks below and read this aloud:

For God so loved _____ that he gave his only Son, so that _____, who believes in him, will not perish, but have eternal life.

Our heavenly Father knows our weaknesses — even before we do — and in spite of them, Jesus died for us out of His great love for us.

Don't ever let Satan make you believe that God will not forgive you. Trust in God's love, that He will never forsake you.

Chapter 10:

FEAR OF MAKING A MISTAKE / FAILURE

Teens Talk

Will (17) shares his fear:

"My parents and teachers call me an underachiever because they think I don't care about succeeding. They think I don't want to try to do anything. I can't talk to them about it because they wouldn't understand.

"I do want to try things, but I'm afraid of making a mistake, of being a failure. It's easier for me to just do nothing than to risk making an idiot of myself if I try something and fail.

"I wish I could just force myself anyway, but I don't know how to stop being afraid. The worst thing is, I'm 17 and will be a senior next year, and I'm scared that I won't even try to go to college."

Jennie (17) responds:

"Making a mistake can be really embarrassing. I've been taking piano lessons for 6 years. My piano teacher could tell that I was embarrassed playing music in front of her. I was afraid of hitting the wrong notes and sounding awful.

"My first recital was horrible. I was afraid to walk up in front of all the students and their parents, and I didn't want to play my song. I ended up crying on the piano bench and then I did something really stupid. I jumped down and ran out of the room.

"It would've been better if I'd just played the song. Nothing was more embarrassing than crying in front of everyone, and then facing them later.

"My piano teacher began to work with me and she said something that really made a difference in my thinking. She said that when someone plays the piano (or does anything), if they play (or do) it timidly, they sound bad through the whole thing. But when they play loudly and confidently, if they make a mistake, it only sounds bad for a fraction of a second. The rest of the song sounds great.

"That helped me to get through many things . . . I'm a lot less timid now, and after you make a couple of mistakes and live through it, you realize it's not going to kill you. It gets easier and easier."

Thad (18) responds:

"It's tough to make yourself do something that puts you outside your comfort zone. I think maybe it's tougher for us because we feel like EVERYONE is watching us. Our parents, teachers, coaches, all adults, and our friends and peers. It's like we've always got an audience, no matter where we go or what we do.

"But sitting back and letting the world pass by is not the

best way to deal with it. I think that's pretty boring. I would rather make a fool of myself trying to do something, than to sit on the sidelines watching and wish I had tried.

"I am not a great athlete, but I had always wanted to play hockey. At first I was scared that I'd look stupid trying to ice skate. Then I was afraid that I wouldn't be able to actually play.

"All my friends played and so I either sat alone on Saturdays, or I'd go watch them play. One day I decided that I looked pretty stupid sitting in the stands by myself, so the next week I suited up and went to the rink to play. It wasn't a game or anything, just a bunch of us guys having fun.

"It was kinda funny. I was all over the ice, sliding, falling, and hanging on to anything that wasn't moving. But I had an awesome time. Once I realized that I could laugh at myself, it was ok.

"Now I'm on the team and I'm a pretty good player! Just think, I could still be sitting on the sidelines if I'd given in to my fear!"

Isaac (16) shares his fear:

"Not to brag or anything, but I'm an awesome soccer player. I was voted MVP at school, and I will probably earn an athletic scholarship. I just love playing soccer. My coach told me about an all star game he wants me to play in. He said that scouts will be there and that I need to play. This is a dream come true, but I'm debating whether or not to do it.

"What if I'm not at my best? What if I think I'm better than I really am? And what if the scout doesn't even notice me?

"These questions keep running through my mind and making me afraid of failing myself, disappointing my coach, my parents, and my school. So many people are pushing me to do this, and so much is riding on it. Don't get me wrong, I know it's a chance of a lifetime. But my fear of screwing up has gotten me down. I'm not sure what to do."

Nathan (17) responds:

"It's okay to be scared, but stop second-guessing your-self. Stop doubting your abilities. Stop thinking so much, and just do what you're good at doing. Sports is a very mental thing. Don't get so hung up on all this other outside pressure. Do what you love to do **because** you love to do it. The rest will come naturally."

What The Bible Has To Say

We wouldn't be human if we didn't experience failure at some point in our lives. It's true — no one is perfect. Only Jesus Christ was without sin and perfect in this world. So, to fear failure is almost an arrogant fear, and it puts a lot of pressure and unnecessary stress on trying to be perfect (which we cannot achieve) instead of being the best we can be.

That doesn't mean that failure is fun, because it certainly isn't. Depending on the circumstances, it can be devastating. But we must go on, we can't live our lives in fear of failure. And we shouldn't hold back from trying something new, or refuse to take risks when the need arises. As Christians, we need to keep our eyes on Jesus and pray that He will help us to do our best, and accept the outcome.

Think of the story of David and Goliath. Now, here's an opportunity for huge failure. An average man is pitted against a huge giant, skilled and trained in warfare, and clothed in full armor.

Under normal circumstances, it would be obvious who would win this battle. But David put on the armor of God. In fact, we are instructed to do the same.

Ephesians 6:10-18 tell us to *"Be strong with the Lord's mighty power. Put on all of God's armor so that you will be able to stand firm against all strategies and tricks of the Devil.*

"For we are not fighting against people made of flesh and blood, but against the evil rulers and authorities of the unseen world, against those mighty powers of darkness who rule this world, and against wicked spirits in the heavenly realms.

"Use every piece of God's armor to resist the enemy in the time of evil, so that after the battle you will still be standing firm. Stand your ground, putting on the sturdy belt of truth and the body of God's righteousness.

"For shoes, put on the peace that comes from the Good News, so that you will be fully prepared. In every battle you will need faith as your shield to stop the fiery arrows aimed at you by Satan.

"Put on salvation as your helmet, and take the sword of the Spirit, which is the Word of God. Pray at all times and on every occasion in the power of the Holy Spirit. Stay alert and be persistent in your prayers for all Christians everywhere."

That is how David was able to slay Goliath and stand up a winner. You are no different than David. Remember that *"I can do everything with the help of Christ who gives me the strength I need."* Philippians 4:13.

How Does This Apply To Me?

Thomas Edison held the world record for 1,093 patents for inventions, including the brilliantly successful light bulb, phonograph, and the motion picture camera. Do you think someone so incredibly intelligent and successful could also have failures?

He did. We'll tell you about three of them.

1. Edison tried to create a market for building things out of cement — things like pianos and houses! Imagine that! It's not hard to believe that idea was a failure is it?

2. He also invented a contraption called the Kinetophone — a very early attempt at making *talking movies*. His contraption (a peep-hole motion picture viewer with two ear tubes for listening while watching images) never caught on, and he gave up on it.

3. For years he tried to find a way to mine iron ore, even selling all his stock in General Electric to fund his experiments. When he finally gave up on that idea, he'd lost all the money he had initially invested in it.

What do you think the world would be like today if Thomas Edison had allowed his fear of failure to rule his life and had stopped attempting anything?

_____
_____
_____

Proverbs 18:15 says, *"Intelligent people are always open to new ideas. In fact, they look for them."* Do you believe that sometimes these intelligent people try ideas that don't work? How do you think they overcome the fear of failure?

_____

_____

_____

Chapter 11:

FEAR OF BEING REJECTED DUE TO APPEARANCE

Teens Talk

Danielle (16) shares her fear:

"I am a 16 year old girl and have a huge crush on a guy a year older than me. He's finally started talking to me and showing me some attention. But I don't know if he likes me the same way I like him. I've seen him talk to other girls the same as he does me.

"Here's the thing: I'm not as pretty as the other girls in school. I'm nice, but I'm fat. I can't seem to lose weight. I really want this guy to like me, and I've tried everything to lose weight. I've starved and made myself throw up, but nothing seems to work.

"I want to be popular and pretty like the other girls so he will like me. I'm tired of crying myself to sleep 'cuz of my weight. I don't want to look at myself in the mirror. If I feel

that way, why would he want to look at me? Please help me."

Phoebe (17) responds:

"I'm 17 years old and about 15-20 pounds overweight. I've tried to lose weight several times, and I'm not lazy. I play ball and do other active things, I just can't seem to lose the pounds that would make me look more like other girls my age.

"Last year I was really depressed about it and was afraid that I would never go out on dates, or be invited to my friends' parties. I started to avoid my friends and didn't go anywhere except school and church.

"My best friend, Casey, got really mad at me and said that I was being unfair to my friends. She said they didn't care if I was bigger than them, she even said that some of the guys at school thought I was cute and had a good sense of humor. She was pretty straight with me and said that I was being unfair by assuming how they felt and ditching them. Man, that made me feel really lame.

"Now I'm hanging out with my friends again, and I've gone out on a few dates. I'm not saying that I'm happy with my weight — I'm not. But I'm not going to let it keep me from enjoying myself and being a good friend to the people who care about me. That's what it all boiled down to — being afraid to be a friend because it made me vulnerable. I'm not doing THAT anymore!"

Sam (17) responds:

"I know what you're talking about, 'cuz I was over-weight when I was 15. The guys in gym class were horrible to me, called me awful names and laughed at me when we dressed out for class. I begged mom to try to get me out of

gym class. I wished I was dead many times.

"Finally mom took me seriously and realized I needed help. She set up appointments with a counselor and a nutritionist. No, we aren't rich, the counselor was from our church and the nutritionist worked as a teacher at our school.

"With their help, I took off a few pounds. I'm still a little overweight, but I have a better attitude about myself now. I've even started teaching a class at church for kids with weight problems. It's amazing, but helping others has actually helped ME!

"Just know that you're not alone, lots of us out there feel the same way. We've got something to offer. We're special too!"

Marissa (16) responds:

"I'm not overweight, I'm too skinny. I have trouble buying clothes because everything is too big and falls off my bones. My best friend is a little overweight, but she's just beautiful to me. The guys think she's a hottie. I think it's because she's so sure of herself. She has so much confidence, you don't really notice that she's overweight.

"I think maybe that's part of the problem. When we think we look different from everyone else, we ACT different because we're self conscious."

Laura (17) shares her fear:

"I get mad sometimes at how much emphasis is put on people looking perfect. If guys are looking for a girl that has the perfect body, and the perfect face, well, that pretty much leaves me out in the cold.

"I'm afraid I'll never meet a guy who will take the time to get to know me and like me for who I am."

Dave (17) responds:

"I can't speak for all guys, but I know how my friends and I feel. Yeah, we look at the pretty girls, but we aren't as picky as you girls think we are. We don't expect you to be perfect. Heck, I don't think I could get a date with a perfect girl — I'm not a perfect guy!

"I don't really care if she's a little skinny, or if she's a little overweight, or if she's blonde, or short or tall. I tend to like a girl if she has a pretty smile and a good sense of humor. If we have fun and laugh on a date, I'll probably call her again."

Marc (17) shares his fear:

"I'm probably your parents worst nightmare. I'm a guy with a nose ring, a tongue ring, black clothes and spiked hair. I started dressing like this about a year ago just for kicks, and now it's just kind of stuck with me.

"I always get funny stares, and then again, I'm ignored a lot, too. Sometimes I see people purposely avoid getting too close to me. The thing is, I'm really a nice guy, but I don't think people give me a fair chance because of how I look.

"If they would get to know the real me behind the garb, they'd find a nice guy who cares for other people. It's hard for me to make friends, and I just want someone to care about me."

Lorna (17) responds:

"Why do you keep dressing like that if it just gets you negative attention? If it's something you like, and it's who you really are, then I guess it's ok, and you can learn to live with how people look at you.

"If you're doing it just to get attention, you're doing a bang up job. But it sounds like you're not getting the kind of attention you really want.

"Unfortunately, most people tend to judge other people by their appearance. Yep, it's unfair, but true. That's why I think it's so important to be involved in some kind of a group activity, like a church youth group. Get involved in something where people can get to know the real you, not just your image.

"Just be sure you don't go with an attitude."

Emily (17) shares her fear:

*"I don't know if I'd exactly say I have a **fear** of being rejected or not fitting in, but it's true, I've never fit in anywhere my entire life. Being rejected and not fitting in is **all** I know.*

*I'm sure I'll never amount to much in life because of my looks. I'm fat and I have horrible break-outs on my face, and I wear glasses. Every time I see myself in the mirror, I hate the person staring back at me. I'm a loser with a capital L. Instead of a scarlet A on my chest, I need a great big L on my forehead. So, no, I'm not really afraid of being rejected — I expect it. I've lived it for as long as I can remember. No one wants to be my friend, and I can't say I really blame them. I wouldn't want to be around me either. But just once it would be nice to **like** the person I see in the mirror."*

Christina (18) responds:

*"Girl, are you down on yourself, or what? Have you ever thought that maybe no one hangs around you because of those huge walls you've built around yourself? It's like you automatically assume what people think of you, not bothering to find out what they **really** think! But you don't*

*get it. **Nobody** is perfect, and believe it or not, there are probably people who would like to get to know you, but you push them away because of your low self-esteem.*

"You need to find your good qualities and focus on those, maybe start a journal. I saw on Oprah once where she said to start a journal and write down one thing every day that you're thankful for. She said that you may have to look hard at first, but write down even the most simple things. Things like the birds singing that morning, or the breakfast you had. If you focus on those things, you'll soon realize that life is beautiful, and so are you.

"You just have to search your soul to find that inner beauty, then the outer beauty will come. You can also know that God loves us all, regardless of our physical bodies. He created us all to be unique. You are special to Him, and He loves you all the time. That's your first journal entry right there."

What The Bible Has To Say

We need to be very aware of the **power of our words**. We wonder sometimes why certain things happen, and why God doesn't intervene, when all the time He's given us *"free speech"* so to speak. We can literally tie His hands with our own **free will of speaking.** That's why it is so important to watch what we say.

NEVER speak negatively about yourself. Proverbs 18:21 reveals just how powerful our tongues are: *"Those who love to talk will experience the consequences, for the tongue can kill or nourish life."*

Think about that. We have the **power of life and death in our mouths.**

Think back to when God gave specific instructions to Joshua for him and his people to march around the walls of Jericho. He told them not to speak the first six times around, and then to praise him the seventh time, and then the walls would fall.

God had a reason for this. It's because he knew that if those people spoke, they would ruin everything. He knew that by the third time around the walls, they'd begin to talk to each other saying things like, **"My feet hurt, and it's hot out here. I'm ready to quit. These walls aren't gonna fall. What was I thinking coming out here and marching around like an idiot."** No, God didn't want that. Those walls would not have fallen if that kind of negative talk had happened.

The same applies to us even now. As soon as we tell someone, *"I'm no good. No one will ever love me. I'm so ugly,"* those words immediately come back to **our own ears.** The longer we repeat those words, and they ring back in our own ears, our spirit will begin to believe it, and what is being said **will begin to take place.**

So instead of speaking bad about yourself, say things

like, *"I'm a good person. Everyone I meet likes me. I have more friends than I can count. I'm special. My beauty is shining through."* And not only will this encourage you, but you will soon begin to notice some changes in your life. And these good things will begin to take place.

James 3:4-6 states it perfectly. *"A tiny rudder makes a huge ship turn wherever the pilot wants it to go, even though the winds are strong. So also, the tongue is a small thing, but what enormous damage it can do. A tiny spark can set a great forest on fire. And the tongue is a flame of fire. It is full of wickedness that can ruin your whole life..."*

So the words we use are **vitally important to us and those around us.**

Also consider this: 1 Corinthians 6:19 says, *". . .your body is the temple of the Holy Spirit . . ."* For that reason, it is important to take good care of your body. That doesn't mean that your first priority should be outer beauty. It does, however, mean that eating healthy and getting exercise should be a part of your daily routine. Use wisdom in your health behavior. It will have a positive payoff.

Our eternal life is so much more important than the value society may place on our lives now. We need to be bold and confident in who we are with Jesus Christ.

And finally, Christ never judged anyone by their appearance. In fact, during His time of ministry here on earth, He treated every person equally the same. He does not base the criteria for acceptance into the kingdom of God by appearance. It is by our faith, love and obedience to God when we ask Christ to enter our heart. And who is more important than Jesus Christ, that we should worry about accepting us? No one.

He will bring true friends into our lives who realize that looks and appearance hold no permanent, eternal value. There is an inner beauty which draws true friendships and lasting relationships.

How Does This Apply To Me?

Have you ever felt judged by your appearance? How did you handle that situation?

_____

_____

_____

What qualities are most valuable in a friend?

_____

_____

_____

What image do you project right now to the people around you?

_____

_____

_____

What is the image you **want to project** to those around you?

_____

_____

_____

How can you accomplish this?

_____

_____

_____

What can you do to improve your overall health? How will this affect your body as the temple of The Holy Spirit?

_____

_____

_____

Do you make negative comments about your appearance?

_____

_____

_____

Now that you know the power your words carry, write down 5 or 6 positive statements you will start saying outloud about yourself.

_____

_____

_____

_____

_____

_____

Chapter 12:

FEAR OF NOT FINDING SOMEONE TO LOVE

Teens Talk

Daphne (16) shares her fear:

"I'm tired of being the loner in the group. All my friends have boyfriends, and I'm the only one who doesn't have somebody. We hang out on the weekends and I feel so awkward being alone. And even when their boyfriends aren't around, my friends still end up talking about them. And again, I feel like the outsider.

"It's not that there's no one I haven't been interested in. But I do have high standards. Maybe too high. My friends tell me I'm too particular, but I can't help it. I'm just worried that I won't find anyone who will be my one true love. Is there really someone for everyone? I don't want to always be alone."

Cherie (17) responds:

"I always hated being 'in between' boyfriends. It was never fun hanging out with 'couples.' I felt like a third wheel. But my best friend pointed out that I didn't have to find my one true love just to go out and have fun. So I began going out with the gang and hanging out with guys and girls as friends. Nothing more, nothing less. And I found myself really having a good time.

"For one thing, there was no pressure, no awkward moments like when you're on a date. We just hung out, laughed and had a good time. And I really got to know some cool guys that way, and we've become really good buds.

"I know I will find the right guy one day. But I can enjoy myself in the meantime. I believe that God has him picked out for me, and I'll meet him when it's in God's timing. Until then, I'm just not gonna worry about it."

Carlie (17) shares her fear:

"I've been hanging out with a great group of friends for about a year now. We're all really tight, we go to movies, to the mall, just hang. Now two of them have started dating and it's starting to feel all weird.

"I kinda feel like I need to find a boyfriend, but there's no one I really like that way. I don't know how to go about asking a guy if he likes me, and I wonder if I will ever find someone who'll like me for more than a friend."

Beth (18) responds:

"It can be a real bummer when all your friends are dating and you haven't found the right guy yet. The conversations revolve around their dates, their guys, clothes for their dates, blah blah blah!

"But hang in there. I've been through it, and trust me, there comes a time when it'll be your turn. I sat around on the weekends while my girlfriends went out, and I sat around the lunchroom at school and listened to them talk about it. Then I met a great guy and we really hit it off, and it was their turn to listen to ME for a while.

"Part of being a good friend is being able to listen and be happy for your friend when things are going their way. Be patient, and keep your chin up. Boyfriends come and go, but good friends are always there, and they are priceless!"

Lance (17) responds:

"My friends and I came up with a solution to this problem, but it takes everyone cooperating and agreeing. There's six of us guys who are close and like to do things together. We decided that Friday night would be 'date night' and Saturday night was designated as the night just us guys would hang together.

"It works great cuz we can all count on the fact that if we don't have a date one weekend, we won't be all alone the whole weekend.

"Of course we'll all go different ways when we graduate, but it's working great while we're in high school."

Tina (17) responds:

"Lance, there's NO WAY that plan would work with my girlfriends. No matter how much we swear we'd hold "Friday night open for just us girls," it wouldn't happen. If they get asked on a date, there ain't nothing short of a world crisis that would make them say no."

Jamal (18) shares his fear:

"Dating can really be a drag sometimes. I really like hanging with my friends more than I do dating because there's a lot less pressure. Sometimes I'm afraid that I won't ever find the right girl because I'm not really looking. Everyone thinks I'm weird because I'm into doing my own thing and not worried about having a date every weekend.

"What if I miss finding the right girl because I'm having too much fun? I don't know how we're supposed to find the right person anyway! It's all very frustrating."

Celeste (19) responds:

"There's no rule anywhere that says you have to be out there seriously searching for somebody. Most of the time we do it because of peer pressure.

"My parents instilled in me from a very young age the ability to think for myself and to be strong in my convictions. I have a goal for my life, and reaching it is going to require a lot of school and a lot of focus on my part.

"I don't want to get sidetracked from getting my degree and a career just because my peers think I should be dating and trying to get married.

"I'm very happy spending my spare time with friends and family."

Damaris (18) responds:

"I don't really feel pressure from my friends to date, it's just that when everyone else is out on a date and I'm sitting home alone with Mr. Fritz (our cat), I can't help but feel a little left out and sad.

"I like your attitude, Celeste. It's good to be so sure of what you want, but what if what you want is to have a date,

and there's no one around that you like? Or even worse, the guy you like is in love with someone else. That reeks, let me tell you!

Ashley (17) responds:

"Love is wonderful and horrible, sweet and bitter, kind and cruel. I write poetry — mostly about love and heart-break.

"My mom says we all want to feel loved by someone special, and most of us will eventually find it, if we don't give up hope.

"So, here's to hoping we all find love!"

What The Bible Has To Say

God wants us to be fulfilled. From the very beginning when God created Adam, He wanted him to have someone to be a companion. Read what God's word says about that in Genesis 2:18:

> *"And the LORD God said, 'It is not good for the man to be alone. I will make a companion who will help him.'"*

There's nothing wrong in wanting to find someone special to love, trust, and share our faith. It's very natural and part of God's overall plan.

None of us know God's individual plan for our lives. We just need to read His Word everyday and seek His face.

If we seek Him and put Him first in our lives, He wants us to have the things we desire. This good news is in I John 5:14-15: *"And we can be confident that He will listen to us whenever we ask him for anything in line with His will. And if we know He is listening when we make our requests, we can be sure that He will give us what we ask for."*

You should pray for a mate who will come in God's timing. Pray that he/she will be a person of strong faith, someone who will share your belief and love for God.

It would be a good idea to pray for this person everyday — even now, even though you don't know who they are.

Pray for their safety, for their good health, and for their daily decisions and choices. Pray that God will bless you with the person who will complete you in Him, at His appointed time.

God's word is true and unfailing. *"Hold fast to your profession of faith without wavering, for He that promised is faithful."* Hebrews 10:23

While you're praying for God's direction, read Proverbs

30:10-31. It talks about the virtuous woman and her characteristics, and what she means to her husband. It describes how she takes care of her family, and how her husband and children love her. It's great reading for both young men and ladies as you seek God's guidance in your life.

How Does This Apply To Me?

How can you pray for God to bless the person who will be your future mate?

_____

_____

_____

How can God prepare you to be a good, faithful mate?

_____

_____

_____

How can you find fulfillment in the meantime with your friends and family?

_____

_____

_____

Chapter 13:

FEAR OF NOT FITTING IN

Teens Talk

Jon (15) shares his fear:

"My parents just told me some terrible news. We are moving. My dad's job has changed, and we've got no choice.

"I don't want to leave my friends. I've lived here all my life, and this is my home. Mom says I'll make new friends, but I don't want to. I want to keep the ones I have.

"I'm afraid of going to a new school and meeting new people. What if they don't like me? What if I don't fit in? I'm worried about it all the time. I haven't told my parents because I don't want them to feel guilty or worry about me. My friends are sad, too, but can't help me.

"How can I get rid of this sick feeling in my stomach and try to get ready for my new life?"

Cindie (17) responds:

"I remember when my best friend told me she had to move. I didn't want her to leave, we'd been best friends since second grade. We sat on the front porch together and cried.

"I didn't really know how she felt until the same thing happened to us. Dad was transferred and all of a sudden it was my turn to have to leave everyone and everything I'd ever known.

"I had all those horrible feelings — wondering if I would find any friends, would I fit in, would I be alone?

"I told my parents how scared and sad I was, and they told me that they felt the same way. I hadn't thought about them leaving their friends, and the house they loved, and a whole lifetime of memories.

By telling my parents, we were able to work through it together. And when one of us started feeling down, we'd pull each other back up.

"Once we moved, we got involved in a church right away. I joined the youth program and started to make new friends.

"I remember having to get to know people. Some of the groups at school were into drinking (which is illegal) and I had to decide whether or not I was going to stick to my personal values.

"It meant that I wasn't exactly popular with that group — but I think they have come to respect the fact that I stand up for what I believe. And I have found friends with similar values and interests. I feel like I fit in now."

Derek (15) shares his fear:

"I just graduated from junior high to high school and because of where I live, I go to a different high school than

most of my friends.

"I have tried to make friends, but no matter what I do, I just don't fit in. Everyone has buddies and there's these little groups, they have private jokes, and it's like I'm not even there.

A lot of the kids smoke and I have thought about starting to smoke if it would help them accept me. My dad would KILL me if he knew I was smoking. I don't know how I'd sneak around and do it, and I don't feel too good about lying to him.

"What can I do to fit in with the 'in' crowd?"

Sasha (15) responds:

"Why in the world would anyone like another person just because they started smoking? And why would you want to be friends with someone who only likes you for a lame reason like that?"

Miguel (17) responds:

"That sounds really smart. Take on an addictive habit that will destroy your lungs, put you in high risk for cancer and heart disease, just to be liked by more jerks who are risking their health.

"Man, take a good hard look at what you're doing. These kids will be out of your life soon, but if you start smoking now, cigarettes could be a noose around your neck for years! That means forking out huge chunks of hard-earned money on three packs a day, forking out even more money on treatments to kick the habit, OR God forbid, doctor bills for lung cancer.

"My advice would be to find you some smart friends."

Teena (16) responds:

"What about the lying issue? How long do you think you can keep smoking without your dad finding out? Then you'll have another huge set of problems much bigger than the first. Smoking is bad enough, but lying (in my opinion) is even worse."

Brandi (15) responds:

"If you'll smoke to get into the 'in crowd' today, what will you do tomorrow when that's not good enough? If you don't draw the line now, you never will."

Tim (18) responds:

"Ok, I'm a country music fan, and I'm gonna quote a line from one of my favorite songs here because it's so appropriate. **'If you don't stand for something, you'll fall for anything.'"**

What The Bible Has To Say

We all want to be loved and feel welcomed, especially in new or different situations. None of us like to feel uncomfortable or alone.

Fear has a funny way of revealing itself, and it's almost impossible to hide. It comes in the form of sweaty palms, armpits and upper lips. Sometimes fear can cause you to cast your eyes to the ground so you don't have to make eye contact. And often it can make you very quiet and shy. It affects people in different ways, but it rarely goes unnoticed by others.

It is important to pray and turn our fears over to God, to pray that He will help us to be ourselves and to be bold in all situations.

He cares so much for us that He will help us to make new friends when needed, or make a sticky situation less difficult. Whatever the case may be, He says in Psalm 32:8 ***"I will guide you along the best pathway for your life. I will advise you and watch over you."***

Have you ever been to a party and felt like a third wheel? Were there people you wanted to meet, but were too afraid to speak up and get to know them? Why do you think you were afraid? Were you afraid of not fitting in, or were you afraid of something else?

On the other hand, have you ever been to a party and wanted to fit in, but didn't because people were doing things that you disagreed with or didn't approve of?

Sometimes we have a feeling that we think is *fear,* but it's really a little voice inside us *(the Holy Spirit)* telling us that we're in the wrong place. We need to listen to that little voice and **always be willing to recognize it** and hear God talking to us. He could be telling us something, like maybe we are trying too hard to fit where we aren't meant to. He could be protecting us.

So, what happens if we are involved in a circumstance where we have prayed for God's help, strength and direction, and yet we still feel uncomfortable? Perhaps then we should consider removing ourselves from that particular circumstance. At the very least, we should look at it closely and consider whether or not being there is in our best interest.

Don't let your desire to *fit in* take over the good common sense God gave you. Always use wisdom and seek God's will in your life.

Remember PROVERBS 4 : 6-8 *"Don't turn your back on wisdom, for she will protect you. Love her, and she will guard you. Getting wisdom is the most important thing you can do! And whatever else you do, get good judgment."*

God cares about all the things in our lives. And even if we think it may be silly to pray before going to a party, He really wants us to come to Him about **all** things, big and small. He cares about everything. Nothing is too small for Him, and He will give you the encouragement and strength you need.

How Does This Apply To Me

Look back at Proverbs 4: 6 - 8. Write down all the different ways you think wisdom can protect you.

_____

_____

_____

In Proverbs 4, Solomon says that if you prize wisdom, you will have a long, good life. How do you think wisdom can bring you a long, good life?

_____

_____

_____

When was the last time you felt awkward, like you didn't fit in? What were the circumstances?

_____

_____

_____

What could you have done to fit in?

_____

_____

_____

How can you recognize when God is telling you that you SHOULD NOT fit in?

_____

_____

_____

Describe the last time you didn't fit in because of your moral values.

_____

_____

_____

How did you react in that situation?

_____

_____

_____

How do you WISH you had reacted?

_____

_____

_____

Chapter 14:

FEAR OF PEER PRESSURE

Teens Talk

Ashley (16) shares her fear:

"Lately a few of my friends have been giving me a hard time because of my values. They like to get drunk and party and say that I'm only young once.

"I'm a Christian and I don't believe in getting drunk, besides, it's not legal at my age to drink. And they give me a hard time because I want to wait for sex until I am married. This is something I feel strongly about, but I've become a target by several friends. I don't want to lose my friends, and while I'm strong in my faith, I'm afraid they will continue to harass me until I give in."

Teresa (18) responds:

"I had this same experience when I went into high school. All of my friends felt like they had something to

prove, I guess, and they started drinking to impress the juniors and seniors. The bad thing was when they all started putting pressure on me to go against my strong beliefs and party with them. They were pretty persistent, and eventually hateful in picking on me.

"My folks raised me to be strong in my values, and I thank God for that. I also had several good friends at church to talk to and lean on for support.

"I kept thinking about a scripture verse we talked about in our youth group ... it was in Proverbs, and it talked about how evil people try to you make stumble and do things you know you shouldn't do, but good friends give godly advice.

*"I had to ask myself if these people were **REALLY** my good friends, would they be encouraging me to do things I didn't believe in? The answer was no.*

"So, I made a tough choice — I chose to find real friends. It wasn't easy, but now I'm a senior in high school and have come through the toughest years. I have a lot of good friends who have stuck by me and love me even if we are different."

Tracie (19) responds:

"People who harass relentlessly until you give up your values are not friends, they are abusers.

*"Find some people who respect your values and care about your well-being. They will be the people who deserve to be called **friends**"*

Zach (16) shares his fear:

"I have a good friend who keeps pressuring me to try drugs. I don't want to do drugs, but I don't want to dump him as a friend.

"Last week, though, we were out together and he looked

in the rearview mirror and started to wig out on me because he saw a cop. We didn't get pulled over, but he told me later that we'd have been arrested for possession.

"I don't want to get into trouble just for being his friend, but it doesn't seem Christian like to dump him."

Brad (19) responds:

"I don't know how Christian-like it is for you to dump him, but I do know one thing. It was WAY UNCOOL for him to have drugs and put you at risk of being arrested.

"And it would be WAY stupid for you to think he won't do it again. Be a friend and tell him to get clean, and do whatever it takes to stay clean yourself. You're too young to get messed up in all that junk and ruin your life."

Jack (18) responds:

"If I was you, I'd talk to my parents about it, or my youth pastor. You can be his friend and try to help him. But you shouldn't be his friend and get in deep trouble just because you don't have the guts to call it like you see it."

Meg (16) responds:

"I don't think a friend should pressure you into doing things you don't want to do. A good friend wants good things for you. And they respect your feelings."

What The Bible Has To Say

Proverbs, chapter 4, is excellent advice when you're facing peer pressure. Solomon is talking to his children and giving them advice — like all good dads do.

Since Solomon is considered to have been the wisest man in the world, what he has to say is probably worth listening to.

Proverbs 4 :14-17 says *"Do not do as the wicked do or follow the path of evildoers. Avoid their haunts. Turn away and go somewhere else, for evil people cannot sleep until they have done their evil deed for the day. They cannot rest unless they have caused someone to stumble. They eat wickedness and drink violence!"*

Solomon repeatedly tells his kids about the importance of wisdom. He must have thought it was a big deal, because saying it once didn't cut it. He goes on and on about how they need to develop good judgment.

He says that wisdom will protect you, guard you, and honor you.

Those aren't words we hear everyday in contemporary society. So, let's think about how wisdom can protect and guard you.

Would you say that wisdom can help you to see things clearly? When friends are pressuring you to get drunk, wisdom will help you to see that doing something illegal can have severe consequences — penalties that could change your whole life. Some of the consequences could include being arrested for driving drunk and having a permanent criminal record; having a wreck and injuring yourself or others, possibly fatally; alcohol poisoning; unsafe sex which has its own consequences; or at best a horrible hangover and being severely punished by your parents.

Wisdom can help you to weigh out your choices and make smart decisions **before you act them out** and can help you to make choices that are **good for you.** It will also help you to see that true, godly friends would not encourage you to do something which is against your beliefs. Instead, they would give you good advice and support your decisions.

It's easy to see how making the right choice at a critical moment can absolutely protect you from harm!

Alright, so how does wisdom *honor* you? It can honor you with a good reputation, which could make the difference as you apply for college scholarships, seek a job, or any other situation where integrity is important. Wisdom helps you to see beyond *right now* and into tomorrow. It honors you with dignity, respect, and integrity. It elevates you to a higher position than those who do not use wisdom. It sets you apart.

Solomon goes on to warn his children with these very frightening words about being led astray by the wicked (which can translate to peer pressure, if your peers are encouraging you to do things that are against your values and your belief and faith in God):

"...The way of the wicked is like complete dark-ness. Those who follow it have no idea what they are stumbling over." Proverbs 4:19

And, finally, Solomon explains about true friendship, which is a good barometer when you're faced with peer pressure:

PROVERBS 12:26: *"The godly give good advice to their friends; the wicked lead them astray."*

How Does This Apply To Me?

We saw in Proverbs 4 that evil people aren't satisfied until they've brought someone else down with them. Let's look at the scripture again, verses 14-17:

> *"Do not do as the wicked do or follow the path of evildoers. Avoid their haunts. Turn away and go somewhere else, for evil people cannot sleep until they have done their evil deed for the day. They cannot rest unless they have caused someone to stumble. They eat wickedness and drink violence!"*

Have you ever been pressured to do something that you knew was wrong? Describe the situation.

_____

_____

_____

When you were being pressured, how did they try to persuade you to go against your personal convictions? What tactics did they use?

_____

_____

_____

Can you look back now and see whether or not their intentions were selfish or destructive?

_____

_____

_____

How did you respond to them?

_____

_____

_____

How can you begin to use wisdom in a peer-pressure situation?

_____

_____

_____

How can you gain the strength you need to stand strong in your convictions and say no in the face of strong peer pressure?

_____

_____

_____

Chapter 15:

FEAR OF TERRORISM

Since the tragic events of September 11, America has come face to face with a new and paralyzing fear — one that our grandparents and great-grandparents never dreamed possible in this great land. Yet, even before the September 11 tragedy, there were the horrifying images from Columbine which terrorized children and parents across the nation. Teens talk about these new, but very real fears and how they are coping with them.

Teens Talk

Mia (15) shares her fear:

"My name is Mia and I'm 15 years old. We've had two bomb threats at our school and I am so afraid. With all the terrorists attacks, I just keep thinking that something awful is going to happen.

"I can't concentrate in class and my grades are starting

to slip. Please tell me how I can go to school without worrying about bombs."

Abigail (14) responds:

"We've had a lot of bomb threats at our school over the past couple of years. It is scary, that's for sure. But I believe that the principal and teachers are doing what they need to do to protect us. For some reason, some people think it's funny and get their kicks from scaring us.

"So I decided not to let them win and I talked to my school counselor. He explained some of the things they're doing to protect us, and it has really helped me to feel safer. He explained that we are well protected and that the students are always first priority. He told me about some security measures that the school is taking, and it made me feel good to hear about it. I'm glad I talked to him.

Hunter (17) shares his fear:

"I'm 17 years old and a senior in high school. I am really struggling with a problem that I'm almost embarrassed to admit. With all the stuff that's going on in America right now, I'm afraid that they might reinstate the draft. I don't want to be drafted!

"I don't plan on going to college, so I would be the perfect age and candidate to be drafted. Is it wrong for me not to want to serve my country? I love America, and I've always thought I was patriotic. But when it gets down to me leaving my home to fight and possibly die, it scares me to death! I feel so guilty for feeling this way, but I can't help it."

Doug (18) responds:

"My name is Doug and I'm 18 years old. I love my

country and I wave my American flag from my American-made Ford truck. I'm not ready to run and sign up to go overseas and fight, but I know that if that's what it comes down to, that God would help me. He would prepare me mentally and physically. And I have to believe that He would bring me back home safely.

"It's only human to be afraid to go to war. I can't help but believe that even the military, who are trained and have chosen that as their profession, have some feelings of fear when they are actually given an assignment.

"We all have fears of the unknown, and war to our generation is basically an unknown. But I believe the Bible . . . if we, as a nation, will turn to God and pray, He will heal our land. So, even though it's normal for those feelings to creep in, I don't think we have to let them control our lives.

"I keep reminding myself that there is no fear in Jesus Christ, and He is the rock that I can depend on daily."

Chris (15) shares his fear:

"My name is Chris, I'm 15 years old. I've been so scared since the trade centers were hit. My parents have the news on tv and radio all the time, and everyone keeps talking about war.

"My dad works in a skyscraper downtown, and I worry about him every day. I wish he could get another job. I can't sleep good cuz I have bad dreams every night. Is it normal for me to want to stay home all the time?

"I feel safe at home, and just don't want to leave. But I know I can't go on like this forever."

Daphne (14) responds:

"I've also been really scared since the terrorist attacks. But my parents wouldn't let me watch a whole lot of it on TV.

I know they don't want me to be ignorant of everything that was going on, but they didn't want me to be frightened either. Mom said that I just didn't need to see the pictures over and over again, and I think she was smart to know that watching too much of it on TV wasn't a good thing for me.

"I like to make jewelry, so instead of watching TV, I spent time making special goodies for friends to help take my mind off all the bad stuff. It really did work, I slowly found myself thinking less and less about the horror and fear of Sept 11, and more about how I could help make people feel good.

"My dad travels a lot, and I was really scared the first time he had to get on an airplane about two weeks after the attacks. But I did the only thing I knew to do, and that was pray. I knew that I couldn't protect my dad, but I knew God could. And He has.

"Once I prayed, I had such a calm feeling, it's hard to describe. Now I pray every day before I go to bed — I ask God to help me sleep and to take care of us, and in the morning before I go to school I ask God to keep us safe during the day.

"It was nice to start every day talking to God and reading my Bible. It has helped me to get back to normal again.

What The Bible Has To Say

With all the news of terrorism and war, it's easy to get distracted from God's Word and His promises to us. Instead of putting all our focus on the news and becoming completely absorbed in it, we need to remember what God said.

The entire chapter of Psalm 91 speaks of how He keeps us safe from ALL harm. Verse 2 says *"He alone is my refuge, my place of safety. He is my God, and I am trusting in Him."*

We can take confidence even further with verse 5: *" Do not be afraid of the terrors of the night, nor fear the dangers of the day. Nor dread the plague that stalks in darkness nor the disaster that strikes at midday. Though a thousand fall at your side, though ten thousand are dying around you, these evils will not touch you."* This is incredible news.

What things in that verse sound like a description of the events on September 11th?

_____

_____

_____

The Lord also says (verse 14), *"I will rescue those who love me. I will protect those who trust in my name."*

Our job is the easiest of all. Love and trust. That's it. We need to be able to turn all our fears over to Him, believing His promise that He will protect us. We have nothing to fear. God is faithful, and will keep His Word to us.

The next time fear of terrorism creeps into the mind, it's important to know the scripture so that we can recall it in our spirit and bind that fear, stamp it **"return to sender"** and refuse to accept what Satan is trying to offer. God is in control . . . **ALWAYS!**

How Does This Apply To Me?

"You will live under a government that is just and fair. Your enemies will stay far away; you will live in peace. Terror will not come near." (Isaiah 54:14) Write down what you think that means for your life as a Christian.

_____

_____

_____

"God is our refuge and strength, always ready to help in times of trouble." Psalms 46:1 If God is your refuge and strength, and He is always ready to help in times of trouble, what can you do to release your fear and trust Him?

_____

_____

_____

Psalms 91:14 says *"I will rescue those who love me. I will protect those who trust in my name."* Read that verse aloud. What are the two things we have to do in order for the Lord to take care of us?

_____

_____

When you are frightened and feel overwhelmed with anxiety, read these words out loud to God until you feel his peace in your heart.

> *"For You are my hiding place; You protect me from trouble. You surround me with songs of victory. The Lord says, 'I will guide you along the best pathway for your life. I will advise you and watch over you.'"* Psalms 32:7,8

Chapter 16:

FEAR OF NOT LIVING UP TO EXPECTATIONS

Teens Talk

Steph (17) shares her fear:

"Nothing I ever do seems to be good enough. I always feel like I'm a failure if I don't push myself to do better than my best. I get so stressed out, and even when I should be pleased with my results, I feel like my parents are disappointed in me. They haven't said so in so many words, but I can sense it in their expressions and their actions. I want to make them proud, but I'm afraid that I'll never live up to their expectations of what they think I should be.

Sometimes I'm so overwhelmed by it all, that I'm tempted to not even go to college. I don't think I could handle the pressure knowing they would be scrutinizing my every move and paying for my education. I wish that I could just be me, and be happy."

Reggie (17) responds:

"My parents are very successful and they have always had huge expectations of me. They always wanted me to get better grades, win all the awards, be better and better, all the time. One award was never enough, there was always the next one waiting to be won. No time to enjoy the victory, time to work on the next competition. I never felt good enough.

It sounds crazy, but I've found that I really love working on cars, and I'm good at it. I'm so good that I have people calling me for advice, like I'm their mechanic or something.

"I don't really know how I learned so much about cars, except that I've always been fascinated by them and I've spent a lot of time taking engines apart and messing with them.

"I started dreaming about opening my own shop. I began to have second thoughts about going to college, but I was scared to death to tell my parents. I didn't want to disappoint them.

"Finally one night I sat down with my dad and told him about being afraid of not living up to what he and mom wanted me to be. He told me that I needed to be like a race horse. I thought **that** *was kind of weird until he explained. He said horses wear blinders to keep them from noticing anything else around them. They just know they have to run the race and run as hard as they can to finish.*

"He said that's all he expected of me. He wanted me to get in the race and do what I love to do. He didn't want me to hold back out of fear of what other people think. And the best part of our talk was when he said he was proud of me for having a dream and wanting to see it through.

I felt such a great release of pressure. I had prayed long and hard about how to approach my dad and that he would be accepting of what I had to say. God gave me the words, and Dad and I had a great conversation."

What The Bible Has To Say

During the course of our lives, there will always be people we will want or need to impress: our parents, teachers, bosses, colleagues, friends, significant other, etc. Does the list ever end? Probably not. But the sad truth is this: If we were to make a list of all the people we strive to impress, very rarely would we see the name *Jesus Christ* on it.

There could be two reasons for this. Ask yourself which applies to you. It could be because we are so busy trying to please other people, we just don't take the time to try to please the Lord. Or, it could be that we believe there's nothing we can really do to **impress** Him, so we don't bother trying. If we were honest, we would probably have to say it's a little of both.

It's true that we don't have to impress Christ, or do good deeds to get to heaven, because we only need to accept Christ as our personal savior and ask Him to forgive us of our sins to ensure our salvation.

However, because we love Christ, it's only natural that we'd want to represent ourselves as He would want us to.

In fact, God set the *Ten Commandments* in place for us to live by. This is a huge responsibility, **but not one to be stressed over.** We all make mistakes, and He doesn't expect us to be perfect. Whew! That's a good thing, isn't it? We just need to do the best we can, and if we fall short, He will always forgive us and will love us just the same.

So, we can agree that although it's important to make a good impression with an employer, teachers, our parents and peers, the best impression is when we have sincerely put forth our very best effort.

Romans 8:1-4 sums it up perfectly, *"So now there is no condemnation for those who belong to Christ Jesus. For the power of the life-giving Spirit has freed you through Christ Jesus from the power of sin that leads to death. The law of*

Moses could not save us, because of our sinful nature.

"But God put into effect a different plan to save us. He sent his own Son in a human body like ours, except that ours are sinful. God destroyed sin's control over us by giving his Son as a sacrifice for our sins. He did this so that the requirement of the law would be fully accomplished for us who no longer follow our sinful nature but instead follow the Spirit..."

How Does This Apply To Me?

Make a list, in order of importance, of folks who place high expectations on you.

_____

_____

_____

_____

_____

_____

Describe the type of things they expect from you.

_____

_____

_____

_____

_____

_____

Do you stress over trying to meet these expectations? If so, how?

_____

_____

_____

How do you think you can rid yourself of this stress?

_____

_____

_____

How do these people react when you fall short of your goals, but have honestly done your best?

_____

_____

_____

If you believe the expectations are unrealistic, how can you communicate this in a positive manner?

_____

_____

_____

Chapter 17:

FEAR OF PUBLIC SPEAKING

Teens Talk

Rob (15) shares his fear:

"I've got to make a speech in front of the class, and it will count as a big percentage of my grade for the year. That's not good because I have a real hard time speaking in front of people. My heart races, I sweat like crazy, sometimes I feel sick to my stomach, and my mouth gets dry like cotton. I hate it. I don't want to do it.

"I know I'll end up reading from the paper in front of me because there's no way I'll be able to look any one in the eye. I'd skip school that day, but eventually I'll have to do it. There's no getting around it. How can I get over this fear? I'll be sixteen next year and I'll have to go on job interviews, and I'll probably have to give presentations in college. I am great at writing papers, but that completely changes when it comes to expressing myself out loud. Help!"

Laura (17) responds:

"I remember something my preacher said one Sunday morning during his sermon. I was one of those people who was scared to stand in front of people and talk. I would get sick on mornings I knew I would have to speak in front of the class at school. When I heard the pastor say that more people are afraid of speaking in public than of dying, I couldn't believe it! I mean, what could actually be worse than dying?? It's kind of stupid to be scared of something that doesn't hurt you, or cause physical danger or pain.

I started trying to understand what it was that made me so afraid of talking in front of people. The biggest thing was that I didn't know WHAT I was going to say. Thinking about standing up there and stammering, stuttering, or worse yet, just standing there silent was what terrified me.

"So, the next time I had to speak in class, I took time to get prepared and made notes to look at. I could actually calm down and not dread it so badly. I was still scared, but I didn't get sick. It still isn't my favorite thing to do, but I'm not one of those people who would rather be dead anymore. Life is too short already!"

What The Bible Has To Say

If you've experienced the fear of speaking in public, you are in good company. Statistics show that this is the number one fear in people of all ages — ranking higher than the fear of death. That means there are actually folks who would rather die than to speak in public. And there are actually those who feel like they are **going to die** if they have to speak in public — but, odds are, they won't. Fortunately, there are some relatively simple steps to help you make it through the harrowing experience should you be required to speak in public.

Step 1. Being prepared is the number one rule. If you are confident in what you are saying, the level of fear is drastically reduced. There is a very simple process to follow for preparation. It's called *research.*

Most likely, you will be given enough notice for adequate time to study your topic. Use the local library, and if you are unsure where to find what you need, ask for help. There is no excuse for lack of preparation. Very few people can just "wing it" and speak fluently with ease, and pull it off. You need to work on what you are going to say.

Step 2. Once you have done the research and prepared your speech, you need to practice it. Find a friend or relative and recite it over and over. You've heard it said that *practice makes perfect*? Well, **practice also makes permanent**, so when you think you've done it enough, do it again. The more you practice it, the more it will stick in your head.

Practice in front of the mirror and look at your facial expressions. Think about what you are saying because it will help you to remember if you think about it **in context**.

Step 3. Whenever allowed, you should have notes. **Do not** read your speech verbatim from a sheet of paper. Instead, have a form of notes, or an outline, that can prompt you to your next sentence or thought. *(Note: Even the*

President of the United States uses teleprompters.)

If you work hard and are prepared, you will feel more confident, and those fearful butterflies will feel less like woodpeckers.

Step 4. Remember that you are not experiencing a rare, unique feeling. There's always a certain amount of adrenalin and nervous excitement before anyone performs in front of a group of people. That's only natural. But the more frequently you do it, and if you diligently follow steps 1-3, the less the apprehension will control you.

Never forget that God will honor your hard work. In fact, Proverbs 10:5 says, *"A wise youth works hard all summer; a youth who sleeps away the hour of opportunity brings shame."*

Proverbs 16:23 tells us that *"from a wise mind comes wise speech; the words of the wise are persuasive."*

Let's make our point, and entice the audience. Being prepared is a powerful tool and can make public speaking much easier.

How Does This Apply To Me?

Describe your first experience of speaking in public.

_____

_____

_____

How did you prepare for this event?

_____

_____

_____

Could you have been better prepared? If so, how?

_____

_____

_____

Chapter 18:

FEAR OF SOCIALIZING WITH OTHER TEENS

Teens Talk

Jaxon (16) shares his fear:

"I'm not exactly a shy person, but I rarely go to any parties even though I'm always invited. I'm never quite sure how to start a conversation with other kids. And even if someone starts talking to me first, I always struggle to think of something to say.

"Sometimes I think I come across as rude or snobby. The real problem is that I just don't feel like I have anything important to say, or that I might say something stupid.

"How can I get past this? I know that to be successful in life I've got to be able to communicate. And I'd really like to be able to go to these parties and have a good time. I just don't know how."

Lindsay (20) responds:

"I used to be really self-conscious and afraid of having any attention drawn to me. When I was in school, I hated to be called up front to write a math problem on the board. I knew people were watching my hands shake and I just wanted to crawl under the desk.

I had a really good youth pastor I could talk to. He was great! He really understood where I was coming from and didn't laugh at me when I told him that even eating in public was sometimes embarrassing and intimidating. He made a suggestion that I thought was crazy at first. But he wouldn't let up! He said it would also be fun, so I tried it.

"Our church school has a drama class every summer — kind of like summer camp. He said I should sign up. I had never done anything with drama because it's performing in front of people. But my youth pastor told me that I was seeing everything as a performance — standing in front of my classroom figuring out a math problem was a 'performance.' It kinda made sense, so I signed up.

The first thing we had to do in class was to stand up, tell our names, why we were interested in drama and what we hoped to learn during the camp. I stood up, I know my knees were shaking, and I thought I'd forget my name. I don't even remember how I made myself do it, but the crazy thing was this. . . the next hour we spent doing some really fun exercises. We all stood up and said tongue-twisters until we were cracking up. We did pantomimes, we did improvisation. And after an hour, I'd completely forgotten I was afraid to speak in public, or have people looking at me. I was raising my hand to volunteer for exercises. It was awesome!

"Going to the drama camp was the best thing I ever did! It helped me to realize that everyone feels the same fears, we just can't let 'em rule us. I'm studying drama in college now, and I have my youth pastor to thank. Thanks, Ken!!"

Philipe (17) responds:

"Man, this is like reading my life! I was exactly the same way, scared to stand up in front of people and do anything. My mom signed me up for a week at the local college. They have summer classes for kids, and the drama class was three hours every day for a week.

"I argued, screamed, begged and pleaded not to go. But my mom is stubborn when she thinks she's right, which is like all the time. She promised that if I hated it after the first day, she wouldn't make me go back.

"It was the most incredible week of my life! The teacher was awesome. She was really cool, and she had us all laughing hysterically from the very beginning. At first, everyone seemed as shy as me, which made me feel a little more comfortable. But it didn't take long until we were waving our hands in the air, begging for her to call on us for the next improv.

"This year I auditioned for a part in 'Joseph' at the community theater and got it! When I think back about how afraid I used to be, I can hardly believe I'm the same person. Thank God for mom, and for a great drama teacher!

What The Bible Has To Say

Socializing at any age can be difficult, but even more intimidating for teens because you are still trying to discover who you are. Sometimes it's hard to talk with new people when you are still unsure of your own identity.

That's why your faith is so important. It's important to always be confident in who you are in Christ, and stand firm for what you believe. Sometimes it's really difficult, but don't be easily persuaded by others.

If you have that part figured out, the rest is a lot easier. If you're faced with an uncomfortable social activity, such as a school or church party, if possible, take a friend along with you. Make an agreement that the two of you will not hide away in a corner, but that you will attempt to meet and talk to new people. With your friend, you're both guaranteed to have someone to talk to when conversation lulls. That will help you not to feel so awkward.

If your friend can't go with you, and you feel overwhelmed with anxiety, don't go alone. Wait until the next party or event. In the meantime, plan on socializing in smaller groups.

When the time does come for you to meet new friends, pray that God will give you the words to say and help you find favor with others.

It's also a good idea to pray for God to give you the spirit of discernment. You want to be able to sense if this is a person you really want to spend a lot of time with. If you feel awkward and your instincts tell you this is not a situation you want to be in, this could be God's way of telling you in your spirit. Never ignore your instincts, always listen to your gut.

Don't lose sight of your faith in order to *fit in* or feel comfortable. You'll be better off waiting to make new friends and socializing elsewhere. God says in Proverbs 4:23

"Above all else, guard your heart, for it affects everything you do." So, stick to your guns, be yourself, and trust that little voice inside you.

Read Proverbs 4:24-27. *"Avoid all perverse talk; stay far from corrupt speech. Look straight ahead, and fix your eyes on what lies before you. Mark out a straight path for your feet; then stick to the path and stay safe. Don't get sidetracked; keep your feet from following evil."*

(Author's note: Drama class or a church youth drama department is a fabulous way for teens to break out of their comfort zone because it's a non-threatening environment and usually a great deal of fun. It's hard to be afraid when you're having fun and laughing.)

How Does This Apply To Me?

What are some of your best qualities?

_____

_____

_____

How can you use these qualities to help you socialize with others?

_____

_____

_____

What are some ways that you could comfortably and confidently introduce yourself to new people?

_____

_____

_____

_____

_____

_____

Chapter 19:

FEAR OF THE UNKNOWN

Teens Talk

Denise (16) shares her fear:

"I'm 16 and think something is wrong with me. I'm afraid to be alone, afraid to go out at night by myself, afraid to go to sleep, basically I worry about all the things that might happen to me. I worry about all the things I can't control — like why my parents might be late getting home, or hearing a report on the radio about a car wreck. I hate being afraid of everything, but I don't know how to stop!"

Leslie (17) responds:

My dad died when I was 10 and it had a really big impact on me. I started sleeping with my mom, which was probably okay when I was 10, but when I got older it wasn't so cool.

"I remember when I was 12, my mom told me that I needed to go back to sleeping in my room. I laid in bed all

night with the lights on and never went to sleep. For weeks I slept with the light on, and didn't fall asleep 'til way after midnight. I was scared of the dark, scared that something would happen to mom if I wasn't with her, scared of someone breaking in the house, scared of everything. Any little noise in the house had me sitting straight up in bed in a panic.

"It got so bad I didn't want to go to school because I was scared something would happen to mom while I was gone.

"Mom made me talk to our school counselor and our pastor about it. She was worried that I wasn't getting any better after dad died.

"Our pastor was really cool. He helped me to see that my fears were worse than any realities. I was conjuring up all kinds of imaginable situations and letting them make me crazy, situations that never happened. It's kinda like 'wait until something happens to get all worked up over it.'

"He prayed with me and sent me home with a book of God's promises — scriptures to help me trust God was going to take care of me. He called me every week to tell me new scriptures to read. I feel much better these days and try not to imagine possibilities of bad things. It's really a matter of trusting God to take care of me and talking to Him every day."

What The Bible Has To Say

Uncertainty is not a comfortable place for anyone. Since none of us can foretell the future, we all deal with the ***unknown.*** That's where our faith in God comes into play. If we trust Him with our **eternal lives**, we should be able to trust Him with our **everyday lives** here on earth.

Life is too short to be concerned with things that may never happen. We need to be able to give our worries to Jesus and let Him soothe away our fears.

Think about when the apostles Paul and Silas were imprisoned (Acts 16:22-40). Back in Biblical times, being in prison was a lot different than it is today. Often the prisoners were executed in horrible ways before they saw the next sunrise. There were no "phone calls," and the prisoners had no civil rights.

So, you'd think that Paul would have been horrified, not knowing how or when he was going to die at the hands of the guards. But no, he trusted God — his Lord and Savior — to deliver him. When an earthquake shook the jailhouse, and the door to his cell was opened, he had the perfect opportunity to escape and run for his life. But did he? Amazingly, no!

When Paul stepped outside his cell, he saw the jailer kneeling with a sword, ready to kill himself because he believed Paul and the prisoners had escaped. Paul told him to stop, and said, "we're all here."

Because Paul trusted God, he not only spared the jailer's life, but he offered him eternal life with Jesus Christ. Paul put aside his own fears and concerned himself with the life of someone else. He trusted God that there was a reason for his imprisonment. In the end, it proved to be saving the jailer's life.

We need to keep our eyes focused on God. Proverbs 3:5-6 says ***"Trust in the Lord with all your heart; do not*** *depend on your own understanding. Seek His will in all you do, and He will direct your paths."*

Another encouraging scripture is Psalm 32:8. *"The Lord says, "I will guide you along the best pathway for your life. I will advise you and watch over you."* It doesn't get any better than that. We are specifically told to seek His will, and trust in Him, and He will take care of us. We have no reason to fear the unknown. It's only unknown to us. God knows everything, and we need to rely on Him to keep us safe.

How Does This Apply To Me?

What is it about the "unknown" that frightens you?

_____

_____

_____

List some ways that you can overcome this particular fear.

_____

_____

_____

Why do you think that God wants us to trust Him in every situation?

_____

_____

_____

Do you believe there's a reason for everything? If so, explain.

_____

_____

_____

_____

_____

_____

Chapter 20:

FEAR OF TRYING SOMETHING NEW

Teens Talk

Janyce (16) shares her fear:

"New things frighten me. I hate having to do new things. Like a new school year terrifies me. I hate new classrooms, new courses, meeting new people.

"There's nothing I can do about it. I know that I would freak out if anything drastic were to happen and I worry about that all the time. I know this sounds crazy, but I don't know what to do about it."

Alex (16) responds:

"New things might seem frightening, but they're also exciting and fun! I used to feel the same way, Janyce, but my

mom set me straight on it pretty quick. She sat me down one day when I was griping 'cuz we were changing churches and I was afraid I wouldn't make new friends. I was really giving mom and dad a hard time about it.

"My mom reminded me of all the times I gripe, saying, "Man, I'm bored!!" and how it always drove her crazy. She said that change keeps things from being boring. If I hated being bored so bad, I should stop avoiding change.

"It made me mad, but she was right. I did hate to leave all my friends at our old church, but I still see some of them at school, and others I invite over to my house. My new friends actually hang out with my old friends and we do neat things together, like hiking and skiing. It's pretty cool.

"I don't think I'd like to change churches again anytime soon, but I wouldn't go crazy if we did. Mom and dad would just have to buy a bigger house to make room for all my new friends."

What The Bible Has To Say

Attempting something new should be exciting and fun. Of course, anxious feelings can also play a role, but don't let fear keep you from trying a new task. You could be missing out on a great adventure if you let fear prevent you from taking any risks. Yes, risks are usually involved, but the great news is that we don't have to face these risks alone. God is always with us.

He tells us in Isaiah 41:10, *"Don't be afraid, for I am with you. Do not be dismayed for I am your God. I will strengthen you. I will help you. I will uphold you with my victorious right hand."*

Think about the fact that God is on our side, and He is always victorious. When Jesus first started His ministry on earth, He went out seeking disciples. He went to each one individually, asking them to turn away from everything familiar and follow Him.

Following Christ would be a completely different life for each of those twelve men. Yet not one of them hesitated or asked for guarantees. They believed that they could trust Jesus, their Lord and Savior, to meet their every need.

You may say, "Well, if Jesus appeared to me, then , yeah, sure I could trust Him and not be afraid to try something new. But I can't see Him." Ok, let's talk about that. Jesus said *"blessed are those who see and believe, but even more blessed are those who believe and haven't seen."*

Did you have the faith to believe He died for your sins on the cross? And did you have enough faith to ask Him into your heart as your Lord and Savior? If so, then certainly you know He can see you through any situation. But you have to do your part, as well. You need to rely on discernment to hear what He is saying to you. We already know that He will direct our paths, but we have to trust Him to do just that. We can't just sit in one spot because we are afraid of what lies ahead.

John 16:13 tells us that the Spirit of truth will show us things to come. So we don't have to feel like we are jumping in over our head when a new opportunity presents itself. Pray and ask God for discernment and wisdom. Then we can cast that fear aside in the name of Jesus, and we can go forward boldly knowing that God will guide us and protect us.

How Does This Apply To Me?

When was the last time you gave up something you really wanted because you were too afraid of trying something new? Describe what happened.

_____

_____

_____

Can you think of anyone else in the Bible who took risks and trusted God to help them?

_____

_____

_____

How did they handle their situation?

_____

_____

_____

How can you apply God's Word to your life to help you release this fear?

_____

_____

_____

Describe an action plan for how you will try new things and work through your fear.

_____

_____

_____

Conclusion:

What I've Learned

Have you allowed fear a strong place in your life?

_____

What does the Bible have to say about fear in general?

_____

_____

_____

List the fears that bother you the most:

_____

_____

_____

_____

What have you learned about those fears through this study?

_____

_____

_____

_____

What does the Bible say about your **specific** fears?

_____
_____
_____
_____

What will you begin doing immediately to conquer these fears?

_____
_____
_____
_____

Write down some goals for the next month to help you overcome your fears.

_____
_____
_____
_____

How was it comforting to hear other teens talking about the same fears you have?

_____
_____

Make a promise to yourself to be more open with your parents about your feelings and fears. Sign your name here to make that promise.

_____

How can you keep that promise?

_____
_____
_____

Make a promise to be true to yourself and stand strong for your personal values by signing your name.

_____

How can you find the strength to keep that promise?

_____
_____
_____

How can these two promises help you overcome your fears?

_____
_____
_____

What resources do you have (after reading this book) for finding help when you face fear in your life?

_____
_____
_____
_____

Printed in the United States
1072300003B/1-30